Terry heard banging.

The last time he'd seen Millard's current project, it had been a six-foot tower of open cylinders, each filled with a rat's nest of colorful wires and coils. It was as if a flying saucer had landed in the middle of the courtyard and then had its outer shell removed.

Terry turned the corner and was instantly dizzy from vertigo. Instead of the small yard he expected, the landscape seemed to go on forever, bending upward somehow, full of mountains and rivers and forests. It was uncannily beautiful, a fairyland untouched by time. But that wasn't the horizon that caught Terry's attention.

Standing a few feet away was a unicorn.

Only it wasn't Horny. No, this unicorn was to the mechanical creature what Horny was to a normal horse. There was no mistaking that he was alive, and yet…

He radiated light, not softly and entrancingly like Horny, but with a sharp and enveloping glow. His mane and tail were also white, but even brighter. His eyes were jet black, as if they opened into deepest space, and his horn was longer and narrower than Horny's but without the curls, sharp and pointed as the tip of a rapier. He turned his head toward Terry, and the sound that came from his muzzle wasn't a whinny but something unworldly, like nothing Terry had ever heard, like every animal combined into one melodious chord.

Terry felt his legs weaken, and his heart seemed to stop for a moment. He couldn't tear his eyes away from the creature.

And then the unicorn was gone. The fairyland beyond disappeared at the same moment, and there stood Millard, with his stained gloves, his torn trousers, and dusty shoes. His face was smudged and his hair was wild, but he looked triumphant. He raised both arms above his head and shouted, "YES!"

"What…was…that…?" Terry managed.

The real Spell Realm," Millard said. "I simply created a quantum bubble, bringing it into our world."

Castle la Magie

by DUNCAN McGEARY

Prologue

Of the Thousand Worlds (there were actually 998 inhabited worlds, but everyone rounded it up), 934 installed the Windford Shield. There had once been 999 worlds, but a single burst of Fanchon Particles from a nearby supernova obliterated Placers Planet and everyone on it.

Fifty years passed before another world was threatened: Spell Realm, which, by coincidence, was the adopted home of Charles Windford himself. What no one knew then was that it was also the home of the young genius Millard Mansing, whose invention was to become even more important than the Windford Shield.

His invention made it possible for Spell Realm to escape the Fanchon Particle burst by shifting it to a parallel universe where magic instead of science held sway. An unfortunate side effect was that because the Windford Shield was used as part of the invention, every planet that had the device was also pulled into this parallel universe.

Nine-hundred and thirty-four civilizations were forced to start over with all new rules.

For most, it didn't go smoothly.

The following is the story of how this momentous change occurred.

Chapter 1

It was my intention that Castle La Magie be a real castle, in form and in function. If, as the guests are meant to believe, there are real dragons, real armies of orcs and goblins, real dangers of every kind, then the castle must protect and defend; it must be sturdy and practical.

I have no desire to recreate the fairy castles of Old Earth. In Spell Realm, there will be no kings or queens, no princes or princesses. Well, perhaps a duke and duchess, or a count and countess, but nothing more than that. Into this world, guests will come, and they will live in times both primitive and dangerous. They will be taken out of their own world and placed somewhere wholly unfamiliar.

We must fight with every ounce of our strength to avoid the frilly, candy-coated Disneyland of legend. Instead, we will create a world with a past both ancient and bloody, where the creatures the guests meet and the enemies they fight are as real as we can make them. They must believe the threats are real, and for that to happen, there must be the possibility of danger.

— Martinique Mansing

"The dragon is malfunctioning again," the speaker on Terry's scooter squawked.

Terry could almost visualize Patrice staring at her fingernails, bored, hoping and waiting for her knight in shining armor to come save her. Even the most unimaginative of them were drawn to the fantasy.

"I'm on it," he said.

She didn't answer.

It was a busy Saturday, especially for the off-season. Spell Realm was packed with day trippers, most wearing the cheapest of costumes. The park's operating license forced it to accommodate local visitors, though almost all the real profits came from off-world patrons.

Terry decided to use the maintenance path to avoid the congestion.

He clicked off the speaker and revved the scooter, doing a wheelie before speeding up the path toward Spell Realm's largest and most lucrative attraction. He'd named the dragon Humbert, and the name had caught on with the rest of the park's employees, except Patrice, of course, who was one of the few people on the planet who didn't anthropomorphize the fairy creatures around every corner, in spite of her longing for a knight.

As far as Terry was concerned, Humbert was a malevolent piece of machinery, always waiting to break down until the park was at full capacity, when Terry was overwhelmed by work. More often than not, what broke would be a tiny, almost inconsequential part, something so small that they wouldn't have it in the warehouse and he would have to rush-order it from off-planet, and half the patrons would have to be comped, the seasonal bonus would be reduced, and everyone would blame Terry.

This was supposed to have been a summer job, but Terry had stayed on through the school year as well, not ready to go back and face his failing grades and miffed parents. He hadn't realized that the park was shorthanded in the off-season and that much of the extra work would fall on his shoulders.

He kind of liked it, though.

He was scooting along at full speed, though official policy was ten kilometers per hour, so when Charles Windford stepped out into the middle of the path, Terry barely managed to swerve out of the way. The path disappeared, replaced by its illusion, a rocky ridge that ran through the middle of the park. A tourist family picnicking below looked up at him with surprise and alarm, and then he veered back behind the digital curtain.

The old man was sprawled on his butt, shouting in pain, his

white hair sticking up every which way, his tortoiseshell glasses askew on his nose. He was dressed in a jester's costume, though his Personage was turned off. Terry had once heard him joke, "If I'm going to be dotty, I might as well dress the part of a fool."

Terry jumped off his scooter and ran to help him up. "Are you all right, Mr. Windford?"

"Of course I'm not all right!" the old man snapped. "I smell oil and gas, and I see a damn scooter and a young man wearing an orange polyester vest, and that is *not* what I'm paying for!"

"I'm sorry, I wasn't expecting you to be…" Terry trailed off, uncertain what to say. *I didn't expect you to be on a maintenance path?* Bad enough that the illusion had been broken without using such a humdrum description. "…to be on a Vanishing Road," he finished, remembering the term used in the brochures in case anyone stumbled on one of the paths by accident.

The Vanishing Roads were one of the few illusions in the park besides the Personages that were maintained by digital effects, along with the physical barrier of running across the top of some rather steep inclines.

The physical manifestation of the fantasy was Spell Realm's selling point and why it could charge more than other parks. Smell, sound, and touch, as well as visuals, were what sold the whole package. Most parks were all illusion, which was far cheaper, but it didn't take much to dispel the effect, especially if you were forced to wear VR goggles all the time. In Spell Realm, you could ride a unicorn and fight a griffin. You could join the rangers to fight trolls or, if you preferred, you could be one of the trolls.

Every kind of fairytale creature was represented in Spell Realm, all of them physical manifestations augmented by digital enhancements.

Terry helped Charles to his feet. The old man glowered, his bushy black eyebrows his most expressive feature.

"Again, I apologize, Mr. Windford," Terry said. *Don't report me!* he wanted to plead. He already had three demerits, and shorthanded or not, park policy was to fire any employee who got five black marks in a season.

Mr. Windford's face softened. "Don't worry about it, young

man. And as I've told you more than once, call me Charles."

"Yes, sir."

Charles was a Perpetual, one of those who lived inside the park's fantasy world full time, as mind-bogglingly expensive as that must be. Terry wasn't sure if he was envious or whether he pitied the old man for living a life that wasn't real. He was also a Centennial, one of the fortunate few who could afford the treatments that extended their lives well into their second century.

Charles sighed. "It's just as well. As a Perp, I need to be reminded once in a while that there is such a thing as the real world." He peered down the concrete pathway, with its dark spots of oil, overgrown grass along the edges, and empty soda can Terry's predecessor had littered and that he kept meaning to pick up. "Ugh," Charles said.

"Let me help you down the slope," Terry said, reaching out. Charles let him take his arm, and they passed through the digital curtain and into the everlasting sunshine of a Spell Realm day. Behind them was what appeared to be a rocky crag, while below was a grassy slope. They made their way carefully down the hill. Charles looked over his shoulder and seemed confused, as if pondering why and how he'd climbed up there. Terry wondered if the old man was finally going completely senile. As soon as his shift was over, he was going to check with the infirmary to make sure Charles was taking his medications.

"I could swear there was a refreshment pavilion up there," Charles muttered. When he turned to Terry, his eyes were crystal clear and sharp. Terry had a vision of what kind of high-powered dynamo Charles Windford must have been in his younger days, the kind of man who could afford to live a fantasy in his later years.

"There are a lot of screw-ups happening, Terrance," the old man said. "Things maybe you aren't seeing…" His voice drifted off, as did his gaze, and when he turned back, he was the old Charles again, his eyes clouded, his voice quavering. "Something's wrong."

"I'll check into it," Terry said to placate him. In truth, he hadn't really noticed, but now that it was brought up, he realized he'd been getting more maintenance calls than usual over the last week or so.

He made sure the old man switched on his Personage, and dithering Charles transformed into a young jester, full of life. Once he was on his way, Terry clambered up the slope, righted the scooter, and took off. He turned on his own Personage, that of a blacksmith, and popped out of the final tunnel-cave, his ride now appearing to the outside world to be a horse.

The tournament arena was surrounded by "Work Zone" and "No Trespassing" signs. Wouldn't want anyone to see Humbert incapacitated.

The dragon was on his back in the middle of the arena, where he'd no doubt been dive-bombing the day-pass holders with digital fire. The dragon burped as Terry approached, flames spitting into the sky. Terry turned off his Personage. It was a distraction when he was actually working. To his surprise, his boss, Carl Lundy, was already there. Carl didn't usually emerge from his workshop until late in the afternoon, after he'd slept off his hangover.

Terry had been amazed to find that no one else had nicknamed Humbert before he arrived. All the other fairy creatures had funny little names. He suspected it was because even when switched off, the Darke Dragon had once been so magnificent that no one dared call him by other than his official title.

Now he was powerless, his footlong scales tarnished and scratched, dull dark greens and blues, exhibiting none of the wonderful luminosity they showed when activated. It was a tradition for each new employee to scratch their name on the back of one of the scales, and the scratches were starting to show.

Terry's full name, Terrance McNally Martini, was scratched near the creature's nether regions, the only place still available after fifty-three years of continuous operation.

Carl knelt near Humbert's head. The dragon's brain case was open, and half the contents of Carl's tool belt were laid out on the grass. As Terry approached, the dragon started humming as if he was struggling to come alive. That background hum was always there, unnoticed by most park attendees, who never got close enough to the dragon to hear it.

"Poor old Humbert," Terry said.

"What's that?" Carl said, looking up at him, annoyed.

Uh oh. Terry had never used the nickname around his boss, and he guessed that no one else ever had either. The Darke Dragon was Carl's pride and joy.

His boss leaned down and switched off the power, gently laying his gnarled hand on the dragon's horned head. "Poor old Humbert," he murmured. "You know, Terry, my dragon never used to hum. He was as alive as you or me. But we all get old, I guess."

"Yes, sir," Terry said, stunned to hear his boss call the dragon Humbert.

Carl stood up. "You wouldn't have believed it," he murmured. He snorted, then echoed the park's motto: "You *will* believe." Terry had never heard it uttered by any park employee without at least a hint of self-mockery, and certainly never with such reverence.

"I met Mr. Windford on my rounds," Terry said. "He seemed to think that we are having more than the usual number of glitches."

"Charles Windford?" Carl said, giving him a sharp glance. "How did he seem to you?"

"Frankly, most of the time he's a little dotty, but there are times when he can be almost intimidating."

"I don't doubt it," Carl said. "But if Mr. Windford is noticing problems…" He frowned, pulled out his workpad, and called up some data. "It doesn't appear we're having more breakdowns than normal, but it does seem like the ones we're having are more serious. It's as if something is interfering with the…"

"With the what?" Terry asked.

Carl looked like he was going to answer, then shook his head. "It's a mystery. Why don't you go ahead and take the rest of the day off, Terry? I'll take care of this."

Since there was an hour before his shift was done, Terry wasn't about to argue.

"Thanks, Mr. Lundy," he said. He turned, anxious to get away before his boss thought better of it.

"And, Terry…"

"Yes, sir?"

"Don't forget to switch to your Personage. Walking around in your work clothes is a sure demerit, and you can't afford another one. I'd go to bat for you, but management is a stickler about their stupid rules."

"I won't forget," Terry said, feeling a little guilty as he realized he'd probably have done just that. Anything out of the routine flustered him until it seemed as if he'd forget his head if it wasn't attached to his neck. "See you tomorrow."

A loud hum filled the air as he left the arena, and bright blue and green lights danced in the sky behind him, lit by dragonfire.

Chapter 2

As much as I might wish otherwise, Spell Realm will not actually be magic (though Flexstone is the closest thing to it). We will be dependent on mechanical and digital effects to pull off the illusion.

However—and this is a big however—whenever possible, we should have physical representations of our world: real animals, real buildings, real trees and rivers and roads.

Sometimes we will need to have both. There is no financially feasible way to create Mount Belladonna, but we can create rough and steep lower reaches so that anyone foolish enough to try to climb it will be discouraged from reaching the area where the digital replaces the physical.

The entire park will require such compromises, but our success will depend on those compromises being rarely discovered.

— Martinique Mansing

The Vanishing Road dipped down the hill and then under it. For the first few hundred feet, Mount Belladonna was a mound of real earth, covered in real boulders. Above that, it continued upward as a digital effect. As far as Terry knew, no one had ever climbed the steep slope far enough to discover the illusion.

Under the mound were the workshop and lockers. It was between shifts, so the vast room was unoccupied. As Terry began to take off his orange nylon vest and overalls, he heard a whinny behind him. He turned just in time to get Horny's wet nose pressed against his neck.

"Hey, boy. What are you doing here?"

Horny the unicorn had gotten his nickname long before Terry had arrived. While he was anatomically correct in every detail, his makers had nevertheless neglected to make certain parts actually work. Despite that, every real mare in Spell Realm seemed to instantly go into heat at the mere sight of him.

Horny's coat was shimmering white, with a contrasting black mane and tail, and his eyes were a deep velvet blue. He was a perfect specimen of a horse. But he was more than that. From his forehead grew a long horn, corkscrewed and shimmering pearlescent white, with a hint of rainbow colors if the sunlight caught the surface just right.

For a while, Spell Realm had had an equine population boom as the stallions noticed Horny's effect on the mares and quickly took advantage of it.

Terry examined the unicorn, noticing his tail last. It hung lank and dead-looking, nothing but tangled plastic. Another one of the little glitches they were having.

"Don't worry, boy," Terry said, patting him on the flank. "We'll have you out of here in no time."

Terry removed a panel at the unicorn's hip and checked the wires. They all appeared to be in place, but... He happened to know there were replacements in stock, so he went to the storage units and grabbed one, then quickly replaced the whole part. Before his eyes, the tail's color deepened and the tangles unwound.

"There you go."

Terry checked the time. Most of the day visitors had already left, but Horny was even more popular at night, when he took on a moonlight glow. Terry opened the door and let Horny out. He whinnied in gratitude and pranced outside, where he was greeted by his harem of mares.

It was impossible not to anthropomorphize the creatures of Spell Realm. At first, Terry had resisted the temptation, but eventually he'd given in, like almost everyone else who worked at the park. Instead of becoming inured over time, most employees became even more spellbound.

Terry trudged to the opposite door, remembering to switch on his costume at the last second, and entered the gated alcove outside the front entrance of the castle/hotel. His quarters were ten levels below, accessible only through the service tunnels. Seasonal employees were relegated to the warrens beneath the castle, but management and full-time employees occupied the back of the first floor of Castle La Magie.

But he had no intention of returning to his rooms. Truth was, he hardly ever spent time there these days.

Instead, he climbed the broad marble (real marble) steps of the castle's main portico, trying to look inconspicuous. His off-duty costume was that of a young knight, one of the most common Personages chosen by male visitors. The only thing distinguishing him, at least to other park employees, was the red patch of a unicorn on his shoulder, the insignia of Spell Realm. If he was caught by management inside the castle without a reason to be there, he could get in trouble, but it was the only way to get where he was going without detouring around the huge structure's outer walls, which would take twice as long.

He glanced over at the visitor's desk and flinched when he saw Granger Hovey, who was the biggest stickler for the rules in all of Spell Realm. Fortunately, Granger was dealing with an obstreperous visitor. Granger loomed over the woman. He managed to be skinny, bald, and vain all at the same time.

"I came all this way to see the Darke Dragon!"

The woman had turned the melodious voice that came with her Personage into a screech. She was dressed in a pink chiffon gown fit for a royal appearance (or a very ugly bridesmaid dress). Yet another princess. She was strikingly beautiful, with long, curling blonde hair and flawless, pearlescent skin, but it was almost certainly an illusion. In Terry's experience, conventionally attractive people often picked more humble, ordinary-looking costumes, no doubt to get away from their normal experience. Unfortunately, for whatever reason, those who chose princess personas almost always had the most horrid personalities.

"I'm sure Hum– the Darke Dragon will make an appearance soon," Granger said, attempting to remain calm. Terry almost laughed, amused that even Granger had adopted the nickname Humbert. "We will, of course, reimburse you for the extra night."

Terry knew from experience that Granger would take his frustration out on his own crew later. Once again, he thanked his good fortune that Carl Lundy had snatched him away when he'd heard about Terry's engineering experience.

A ballroom occupied most of the back part of Castle La Magie. Filled during the day with sofas, chairs, and tables, it was nonetheless empty of visitors more often than not. There was something about the cavernous space that seemed to repel people. Before he'd met Shara and Millard, Terry had spent a lot of time there reading, undisturbed.

A digital bookcase hid the back exit. Terry looked around to make sure the coast was clear and then walked through the illusion.

The back of the Castle La Magie was as plain and ordinary as could be, complete with cinder blocks and metal struts, and no landscaping. Instead, there were expanses of weeds and grass, with cattle, horses, and other live animals dotting the open fields. No fences were necessary, as the area was enclosed by the digital illusion of sheer cliffs, though in fact, there were deep canyons beyond the curtain, without air, as cold as space. Once in a while, an unfortunate animal would wander off the edge, but since they had a surplus, no one did anything about it.

Shara had started a project of putting up fencing, but it had proven too big a task. Still, every once in a while, especially after one of her pets disappeared, she'd get active again, lassoing Millard and Terry into helping her put up barriers.

Warehouses and workshops dotted the landscape in no particular order. One of the smallest warehouses was near the border, only a few dozen yards from the hidden abyss. Terry always worried about that. Millard could be so absent-minded, so absorbed in his experiments that he didn't watch what he was doing or where he was going. And he spent most of his time in his laboratory workshop, which was even closer to the edge.

Terry heard banging and headed that way. Except when Millard was sleeping (and sometimes even then), he was always in the workshop.

The last time he'd seen Millard's current project, it had been a six-foot tower of open cylinders, each filled with a rat's nest of colorful wires and coils. It was as if a flying saucer had landed in the middle of the courtyard and then had its outer shell removed.

Terry turned the corner and was instantly dizzy from vertigo. Instead of the small yard he expected, the landscape seemed to go on forever, bending upward somehow, full of mountains and rivers and forests. It was uncannily beautiful, a fairyland untouched by time. But that wasn't the horizon that caught Terry's attention.

Standing a few feet away was a unicorn.

Only it wasn't Horny. No, this unicorn was to the mechanical creature what Horny was to a normal horse. There was no mistaking that he was alive, and yet...

He radiated light, not softly and entrancingly like Horny, but with a sharp and enveloping glow. His mane and tail were also white, but even brighter. His eyes were jet black, as if they opened into deepest space, and his horn was longer and narrower than Horny's but without the curls, sharp and pointed as the tip of a rapier. He turned his head toward Terry, and the sound that came from his muzzle wasn't a whinny but something unworldly, like nothing Terry had ever heard, like every animal combined into one melodious chord.

Terry felt his legs weaken, and his heart seemed to stop for a moment. He couldn't tear his eyes away from the creature.

And then the unicorn was gone. The fairyland beyond disappeared at the same moment, and there stood Millard, with his stained gloves, his torn trousers, and dusty shoes. His face was smudged and his hair was wild, but he looked triumphant. He raised both arms above his head and shouted, "YES!"

"What...was...that...?" Terry managed.

"The *real* Spell Realm," Millard said. "I simply created a quantum bubble, bringing it into our world."

"*Simply created...*" Terry had always known that Mill was a genius, but this was beyond all imagining.

"That was Horny as he really exists," Millard said, shrugging as if it was no big deal. "Everything you can imagine exists somewhere in the quantum universe, Terry."

Terry stared at him, and for the first time, Millard looked uncomfortable.

That is, the real Millard did.

There was another Millard standing behind him who was smirking.

Two Millards.

Chapter 3

My husband's inventiveness did not stop with Flexstone, of course. The nanotechnology inherent in the building material can be adapted to any number of uses, once one understands the basic principles. But the more objects exposed to the outside world, the more danger there is that others will be able to reverse-engineer the process, and that we must avoid at all costs.

We have made more money than we could have ever dreamed by allowing Flexstone to be sold as building material, but only as building material. So far, no one has been able to figure out how Halor did it.

I occasionally see our competitors' spies in Spell Realm. No matter how hard they try to disguise themselves as tourists, they are usually quite obvious. I see them prying up parts of the roads or pulling hair from the unicorn's tail (and more than one has been kicked in the chest for their efforts). But our sensors know when someone is trying to leave with our licensed technology, and they leave empty-handed.

— Martinique Mansing

Caleb Chance followed Shara through Castle La Magic as if he was her familiar. Which was the right word, because he was far too familiar, constantly invading her personal space with his overattentiveness. He was tall and skinny, but not bad-looking in his own gawky way. His Personage was that of a lowly hedge knight, but she knew that he was high up the ladder in the Morgana Corporation.

Nobody was supposed to know that Lady Shara was in actuality Sharina Mansing, the daughter of Spell Realm's founder. But Caleb was constantly hinting that Shara was more important than the clerk she pretended to be.

Then again, he probably acted that way with all the female staff.

"You have been a fine guide, Lady Shara," Caleb said, seemingly just inches from her ear. She almost shuddered but managed to turn to him with a smile.

"Thank you, good sir, but I am not of noble blood. You may call me Shara."

Caleb gave her a knowing look. "I have no wish to take advantage of my position." He said it as if he meant the opposite. "But, if you would be so kind, I would like to ask the favor of your company for dinner tonight."

"Oh, that would not be at all proper, sir," Shara said, putting on the complete act, even managing to blush. She sometimes marveled at her own acting ability. It was said that her mother had been similarly talented. "I'm sure they wouldn't so much as let me into the banquet hall, even if I had anything proper to wear."

"If I have the food delivered to my room, I'm certain any attire you should choose will be more than good enough."

Or no attire at all? she almost shot back.

Shara wondered how close her father expected her to get to Caleb Chance. Close enough to find out what he was up to, but surely not as close as this man wanted.

Her father had called her into his office late the night before. She'd ignored his summons until she was sure most everyone was asleep and that she wouldn't be noticed when she slipped into his tower's elevator.

She wasn't surprised that her father had summoned her at such an hour. Halor Mansing seemed to never sleep. When she stepped into his office, he looked up tiredly from his desk. Shara had asked him several times what his current project was, but for once he was being tight lipped. Whatever it was, it was wearing him down.

"Sharina, I have a job for you," he said.

She went around his desk and kissed him on the cheek. "And greetings to you, too, Father. I'm doing very well, thank you."

He leaned back in his chair, a reluctant smile coming over his face. "Still dressed as a servant. Doesn't everyone see through that guise?"

"You forget, Father, that I was away at school for longer than most of your employees have worked for you." *Not to mention I'm six inches taller and have, well, a few more curves.*

"You are to the manor born, Sharina. You can't possibly be fooling anyone."

"You'd be surprised, Father. I have a knack for pretending."

He examined her seriously, his smile gone. Then he nodded and murmured, "Just like your mother."

She nodded back. "So it would seem."

He rubbed his eyes, then looked around as if forgetting why he'd called her. He glanced down at a paper on his desk and sighed.

"Well, I'd like you to use your guile on a visitor tomorrow. He is supposedly on vacation, but he works for a company that has in the past tried to spy on us. Mr. Chance hasn't hidden his identity, so my worries may amount to nothing, but I'd like to keep an eye on him."

"Don't you have people for that?"

"None with your abilities to…pretend," he said.

"What can I do?" she asked, genuinely curious. It was the first time her father had ever asked her to do anything like this. He'd been a little exasperated when she'd informed him on her first day back that she wanted to be incognito, but he'd reluctantly agreed.

"Just keep him company and see what he's up to," he said. "But don't challenge him in any way. Caleb Chance has the title of vice president, but I haven't been able to figure out what he actually does for Morgana Corp. He's due to arrive a ten o'clock tomorrow morning."

Shara shrugged. She wasn't sure what she could discover that way, but it didn't seem like a difficult task. It wasn't all that different from her regular job of escorting VIPs around Spell Realm. As it turned out, Caleb Chance had wanted to see the usual sights and had constantly referred to a list that he'd downloaded—nothing nefarious, except perhaps his intentions toward her.

Shara came back to the present, realizing that her shift was coming to an end. Guests were on their own after six o'clock in the evening. She decided to risk dropping the act.

"I have a previous engagement, Mr. Chance. I'm very sorry."

He looked surprised, then bowed. "I understand, Miss…"

"Shara, just like my Personage. It's been a pleasure, Mr. Chance. Please don't hesitate to ask for me again."

"Oh, I will," he said.

Shara began to turn away.

"Wait, Shara."

She turned back, a polite smile on her face. "Yes?"

"I believe it is appropriate to tip the help for services. What do you usually get?"

"That won't be necessary," she said. Right now, she wanted nothing more than to get away from Mr. Caleb Chance, who was starting to seriously annoy her.

"Would a hundred be enough?"

Admittedly, it was a nice tip, more than she usually got, and if she was truly Shara the clerk, she'd be delighted. She managed to put on a smile and took the money. Then she walked away, not looking back. She could feel his eyes on her all the way to the corner.

Caleb Chance watched Shara—whom he knew to be Sharina Mansing—turn the corner of the hallway and disappear. He sighed. He had known from her pictures that she was a lovely young woman, but she was even more impressive in person. But she'd taken an immediate dislike to him, and everything he'd tried to change her mind had only made it worse.

Nevertheless, he'd been with her long enough to see that she was unguarded. Indeed, as amazing as it seemed, none of the people they ran into, including the fellow employees she must see every day, knew who she really was.

Astounding.

She would be easy to kidnap, if that's what they decided. Personally, he thought the whole thing was a mistake. Halor Mansing had enough money to buy Morgana Corp. ten times, a hundred times, a thousand times over. But despite his title of vice president, Caleb was little more than an errand boy and had little say in these things. He had lucked into his job, having helped save the daughter of Morgana Corp.'s CEO from muggers. In truth, he'd done almost nothing: took a few swings at them, took a few punches in turn, kept them occupied long enough for the police to arrive.

One thing was for sure. He wanted to be out of this fairyland nonsense before they took her. Caleb had a feeling that Halor Mansing wouldn't take it well.

Chapter 4

Inventors need looking after. They are perfectly capable of appearing at breakfast having forgotten to put on their pants after inventing something the night before that would change the lives of millions.

My first date with Halor was a favor to a friend. I'd seen him around campus, his head buried in his workpad as he walked around the commons, bumping into people, apologizing unconvincingly, then walking on while typing furiously.

The dinner wasn't going well. We couldn't seem to find a subject to talk about. The nadir of the evening was when he spilled a glass of wine on my lap.

Then, suddenly, Halor snatched the napkin out of my hand, excavated a pencil from his coat pocket (I'm not sure I'd ever seen a pencil before that), and started jotting down algebraic equations on the napkin, then folded it and put it in his pocket. It seemed that only then did he remember that there was a woman sitting across from him.

"What did you just write down?" I asked.

He looked down at his dinner plate, blushing furiously. "I thought of a type of glass that won't tip over," he muttered.

I laughed, then realized he was serious. I reached out and covered his hand with mine.

"Explain it to me."

— Martinique Mansing

Millard never expected the experiment to be a success on his first try. He'd built the machine as a prototype; if anything happened, he expected it to be in the microscopic realm. Then again, he'd decided long ago to never think small, so he'd programmed it for the possibility of something bigger.

The machine was a claptrap affair, made from spare parts and odd found pieces, shaped by an intuitive design that Millard himself could only partially explain.

He'd stayed in the workshop the night before, too excited to really sleep but managing a few winks before waking up at dawn. He got up, slipped on his shoes, and hurried to his desk.

"Coffee," he said.

A drawer opened, and a steaming cup of coffee appeared to levitate into the air. Millard snatched it and then frowned at a faint mechanical whirring sound. No matter how hard he tried, he hadn't been able to eliminate that sound, which detracted from the magical feel. It offended him somehow, as if it meant that the park was nothing but a big con.

Spell Realm needed to be real. *Why shouldn't it be real?*

Everything in the workshop was designed to look old-fashioned. Of course, the entire park was built with the same illusion in mind, but Millard took it a step further, hiding every sign of the mechanical. His desk was littered with papers, pens, and pencils. Underneath all the clutter was his workpad, on which most of the real calculations were done, but he liked the feel of paper whenever he could get his hands on it. Fortunately, he lived in a place that pretended to be magical, so for appearance's sake, Castle La Magie actually utilized real paper. Much of the office work in Spell Realm was done with techniques that the outside world had abandoned long ago.

His favorite thing was the big leather-bound book he'd found in the warehouse. It was meant to be a Castle La Magie ledger, but he'd pilfered it when no one was looking. He'd filled it with his grand plans, all of which were inspired by magic, even as they were underpinned by science.

He liked to think of the ledger as his grimoire.

He opened the grimoire, mentally checking his final estimates, determined as always not to use his workpad. Of course, that was nearly impossible, especially for an experiment as complicated as this, no matter how intelligent he was.

And he suspected that there were few if any living humans who were as smart as he was—except, of course, Halor Mansing.

It was ironic that Millard was so suited for science when what he really wanted was magic. Equally ironic, it was his scientific knowledge that had brought him to this magical place.

On his home world, a drab engineering world where the ethos and aesthetic were technological, he'd shown his aptitude early. He'd quickly surpassed his high school teachers, so he had become the youngest-ever college student, and that had been exciting for a while before he discovered he also understood more than his college professors.

His mother had no idea what to do with him. He had no friends. It was a lonely existence, which he filled by reading every fantasy book he could find. He dreamed of visiting Spell Realm, but his mother could barely afford the basic necessities and rent on their small apartment.

Then, one day, he'd heard that the great Halor Mansing was holding a contest. The prize was an all-expense-paid two-week trip to Spell Realm. It was meant to be a creative exercise; to guess how Flexstone was made. Of course, no one was expected to figure out the answer. A generation of scientists and experimenters had attempted to reverse engineer Flexstone, and none had come close to succeeding. There were inferior brands on the market, but in the end, most people chose Flexstone.

But Millard had come at the problem from a different direction. Instead of trying to figure out how Halor Mansing had invented Flexstone, he'd decided to approach it as an alchemical experiment, as if it was pure magic. Then, with the basic method worked out, his brain had started supplying the equations to prove it.

He'd sent his thesis off, never expecting anything to come of it.

Then Halor Mansing himself had come to Millard's world to declare him the winner. A worldwide celebration was declared—one of their own had impressed the most famous inventor alive—and it wasn't until late that night, after everyone had gone home, that Millard found himself alone with the great man. His mother had hovered around the two of them all day, but finally, nervous exhaustion had sent her off to bed.

They sat at the old round oak table in the tiny kitchen.

Millard was embarrassed by his surroundings. He suspected that Halor Mansing's suit was worth more than everything they owned.

"Tell me how you came up with your solution," Mansing said. He was a trim, middle-aged man with a sharp goatee and curling mustache that were just starting to turn gray.

Millard asked the question he'd been dying to ask all day. "You mean it was correct?"

Halor searched his face, as if wondering if Millard was pulling his leg. "Not in the slightest. I read your proposal and almost tossed it on top of the pile of rejects, but something about it caught my eye. I gave it to one of my people and asked them to see what they could do with it. She came back with something that worked almost the same as Flexstone but wasn't Flexstone. In some ways, your formula is an improvement."

Halfway through Halor's response, Millard was wracking his brain trying to remember what agreements he'd agreed to sign. They had needed his mother's signature anyway, so he'd let her take care of it. No doubt, she'd given it all away. But who was to know?

Halor smiled and sat back. "You really are different. Most young men your age wouldn't think to wonder about the ramifications of what I just said, but I can see your brain whirling. But don't worry. Your formula is unworkable for several reasons. The most important is that the materials required would make your invention prohibitively expensive, and another is that your product would decay after a few years. Nevertheless, I am enormously impressed. No one else has even come close."

Give me a chance and I'll improve it, Millard thought.

"There you go again, thinking of the angles," Halor said. "But I'm here to offer you a contract for your formula. There are parts of it I can use. Technically, I already own your invention, as you've no doubt guessed. But I'd rather have you on my side, Millard. How do you feel about coming to work for me?"

"On Spell Realm?"

"Of course; that's where I live. I'll give you and your mom free room and board, as well as giving you a generous salary."

There wasn't the slightest doubt that Millard would accept,

but he attempted a frown. "I'm not done with school."

"Oh, yes, you are," Halor said. "If anything, you should be teaching the classes you're attending. But let me sweeten the deal. If you come work for me, I will give you your own lab with everything you need."

Millard opened his mouth, but nothing came out.

Halor continued as if he'd said yes. "Now...you didn't answer my question. How did you arrive at the formula?"

So Millard and his mother had come to Spell Realm, and for the first few months, Millard didn't even go into his lab. He took advantage of every adventure the park had to offer, and at first, that had been more than enough to keep him occupied. Eventually, he began to notice that no matter how hard Spell Realm tried to appear magical, the science beneath was always evident—at least to Millard.

And that got him thinking.

He'd headed to his new lab and started working.

What he hadn't foreseen was that his mom and Halor Mansing would get along. He started seeing them together but didn't think much of it until he arrived home early one evening to hear telltale bangs and bumps from upstairs, and then marching down the stairs had come Halor Mansing. He looked as businesslike as ever, but it was impossible to ignore that his shirt was askew and one of his shoes was untied.

To Millard's amazement, shortly thereafter, his mom and the great inventor had married, making Millard the stepson of one of the most famous men in the universe.

It would have gone to his head if he hadn't been so busy working.

The problem, as he saw it, was that Spell Realm was based on science. What it really needed was magic...*real* magic. Of course, physics didn't allow that, at least not in this universe. But if, as most scientists now believed, there were infinite universes, then why not tap into one of them?

His first invention had been what he called his fantasy lens, which allowed him to see into other dimensions. That alone would have made him instantly famous if he'd bothered to tell anyone about it. Instead, he'd spent months exploring new worlds, most of them completely inhospitable to humans, some of them even more mechanistic than his home world, and a few of them impossibly surreal.

When Millard found worlds where the physics allowed magic, he had to decide if that magic could be believed in this world. Most were too fantastical, or not fantastical enough, but eventually he found a parallel world that had just the right amount of magic.

His next task was to find a way to bring a quantum bubble of that world into his own reality.

When he finally turned his machine on, it whirred and cranked and belched. Wires melted and coils seized; smoke curled above the contraption. He took a wrench and slapped it down onto the top plate.

The air shimmered, and Horny the unicorn pranced out of the smoke.

Only it wasn't Horny.

Horny was pretty, but this creature shone with magic. It pawed the ground as if ready to attack, and then the machine ground to a halt.

"Yes!" Millard shouted, pumping his fist in the air.

Behind him, he heard Terry gasp, "What…was…that?"

Millard excitedly tried to explain, but in the middle of his explanation, his best friend's mouth fell open.

Millard turned—and looked at his reflection in a mirror. But the Millard in the mirror image was wearing a wizard's conical hat. Millard didn't own a hat.

His next thought came as if from somewhere else: *There is no mirror in my lab.*

Chapter 5

The Perpetuals were a big surprise to me. It had never occurred to me that anyone could be so rich that they could live every day in the magic of Spell Realm. But of course, given the choice, who wouldn't?

At first, I was opposed to the idea, and I proposed limiting visits to several months. Halor talked me out of it, saying that we couldn't afford to forgo the guaranteed income. Over time, I began to realize that the Perps were actually a benefit to the park. Many of them had great charisma and authority, as befitted someone who had become ultra-rich in their younger days. They became legendary in their own right. Guests sought them out.

The longer the Perps lived in the fantasy, the more invested they became. The more invested they were, the more convincing they were to others.

Some Perps have been here so long that the anti-aging formulas have started to become less effective, and some of them are indeed convinced that the illusion is the reality.

Mostly, I have left them alone. But sometimes I seek them out, enjoying their delusions and wishing I could be so immersed in something.

— Martinique Mansing

The two moons were full, visible in the green skies even during the day. Mill had been tracking the unicorn for a week. The forest was dense, and branches constantly knocked his hat off. He should have left it at home, but he felt naked without it. It was a symbol of his status—or more accurately, it was who he was.

Spells were particularly unreliable when it came to this most magical of creatures. He doubted Lumbli would approve of his student even trying one. "You're not ready," he could hear his mentor say.

You're not ready. Mill heard those three words first thing in the morning and last thing at night; he heard them in his dreams, and he heard them even when they weren't spoken.

But how often did a Majestic Ultima pass through this province? Had it ever happened before? Would it ever happen again?

Mill doubted it.

You're not ready. But by the time he *was* ready, it would be too late. He'd be a tottering old man like Lumbli, too feeble to even make the attempt.

The unicorn wasn't trying to hide. It was so powerful that it warped the time and space around it, so that anyone who approached it felt a sudden impulse to turn away, remembered a vital task that needed doing, or simply lost interest, sometimes wondering why they were even there.

It took all of Mill's willpower and concentration to follow the path. In time, he learned to go in the direction he didn't want to go, the one that made the least sense. This contrary approach proved the most reliable tracking method of all.

And finally, he stood on the edge of a glade where the unicorn was drinking from a spring, its horn stirring the waters into a whirlpool. The colors were more vibrant than any Mill had ever seen; the blue of the water, the green of the grass—it was as if they were new colors, never before witnessed by living eyes. The unicorn itself rippled with color, reds as fresh as blood, yellows brighter than fire, purples so deep and rich they were no longer purple but something new altogether.

It was overwhelming. Mill closed his eyes, trying to stay in the moment, afraid he'd wake up and find it was all a dream.

He fell backward onto soft grass.

A single pebble, no bigger than a fingertip, struck his tailbone, and it hurt just enough for him to open his eyes, to stare at an unfamiliar sky, with moons and stars he'd never before seen. With all the ambition he'd ever possessed, which was more than any other human he'd ever met, he sat up, just in time to see a small strand of the unicorn's mane fall into the grass. He crawled toward the tuft of hair, unable now to look at the unicorn itself.

His fingers clutched the white strands, which turned into all the colors of the rainbow in his hands; magic that turned into colors he recognized.

He chanted the spell, the one he'd learned long ago against his master's wishes. The words formed on his lips, but alas, they were without force or power.

"Magic of the horn," he began. He felt dizzy and closed his eyes, then forced himself to continue. "Magic of the horn, capture this place, hold this moment, place it in my hands, and let it be forever mine."

He forced himself to open his eyes again, certain he'd failed. The glade glimmered and shifted. The unicorn had disappeared, and it was as if a dreadful tapestry had fallen over Mill, woven by the worst weaver in all the realm, a talentless, colorblind artist who could but mimic his betters.

Strangely, he saw himself in this reflection. Into this dull and spiritless place, Teric entered the glade from the side opposite Mill. The servant was dressed like a nobleman, but a strange combination of squire and knight, as if he was costumed upside down for Queen Margot's Ball.

Mill's ghost reflection and Teric exchanged a few sentences that made no sense to Mill. The language was almost familiar, with magic words like "quantum" and "entanglement," but the rest was gibberish. They didn't notice him at first, and then Teric saw him and his mouth dropped open.

Mill smirked, for the servant was no doubt dazzled by his accomplishment. Like the great wizards of legend, he'd acquired unicorn magic. Though it appeared to have drained the very landscape of life and color, he had made the hair of the unicorn his.

But where was the unicorn?

Mill's reflection turned around. His own amazement was mirrored in his double's eyes. That's when he noticed that this doppelgänger was wearing an outlandish costume, something like a blacksmith's apron. Only then did he believe what he was seeing.

"What…wh-who…" the doppelgänger stuttered. Mill sensed that the creature hadn't spoken in any language he'd ever heard, but because of the unicorn's magic, and because this place was now his, he was beginning to understand the words.

The double spoke again, and Mill cast a translation spell. As he made the last gesture, he felt the magic around him disappearing. He staggered, feeling as if someone had removed something from deep inside him with a knife.

"Where's the Majestic?" Mill demanded.

"The what?" the double answered.

"The Majestic Ultima."

"The unicorn?" Teric asked.

"Be silent, Teric," he said, casting a silencing spell on the servant. To his amazement, Teric kept speaking. He didn't even bat an eye.

"It's gone. It disappeared when you showed up, pal. Was that some sort of new digital effect, Millard?"

Millard?

His double answered. "It was real, as real as…" he gestured toward Mill. "I believe this is *me* in the other universe. Somehow he was caught when the experiment failed."

This was intolerable. This mirage was saying that *he* was real and *Mill* the illusion!

Mill wove his hands in the spell that had taken the longest for him to learn, one that Master Lumbli had warned him to use only when he was in the utmost danger. The banishment spell curled from his hands and floated about the double's head.

"I've got to leave," the false Mill—*Millard, was it?*—blurted. Then he looked confused and glanced at Teric's double, as if the servant had the answer. False Teric shrugged.

Mill was dismayed and yet somehow encouraged. Unlike his silencing spell, this one at least had had an effect. But the spell's weakness was especially dismaying because Mill could feel the unicorn's magic coursing through his veins.

"So…how do we send him back?" the false Teric asked.

"That would be impossible," the false Mill said. "I'd have to create the exact same conditions, down to the quantum level. However," he cocked his head and squinted, a gesture Mill had seen a thousand times in the mirror. "I could send him to a probability that would be so close to his own that the differences would be virtually unrecognizable. Of course, he might not be wearing a bathrobe," the double said, gesturing toward Mill's wizard's cloak. Mill was insulted—it was best cloak at he owned, his level-five red cloak that was the only one in all the province.

"Enough!" Mill said. "I will find the Majestic Ultima again and return to my home."

"Yeah," Millard said. "About that..."

Chapter 6

Flexstone: Such an inelegant name for such an elegant invention.

Most of the inhabited worlds have access only to the basic building block my husband originally envisioned, but even that is magical. When Halor first proudly showed it to me, it was a simple square block, made environmentally friendly through nanotechnology. He saw no further than that it could be used in any climate to create structures that could be assembled by anyone.

But I quickly realized that the shape of the block was flexible. It could be tall and narrow or short and wide. It could be thick, or it could be thin. Laid directly upon the ground, it could become more level than any concrete foundation.

The size and shape of a Flexstone building was limited only by imagination. Even the cost could be overcome, for one Flexstone could be purchased at a time, and over a lifetime, a mansion could be built by even the most humble of builders.

It changed everything, made everyone's home a castle.

But that was only the beginning.

— Martinique Mansing

Terry felt a breeze blowing toward the nearby vacuum. When he looked up, he saw that the clouds were feathering rapidly. There were smaller containment fields dotting the realm, but above them, the atmosphere was rapidly disappearing.

Not for the first time since he'd come to Spell Realm, he thought, *What's Millard done now?*

The alarms had started sounding the moment his friend had stopped speaking. They were the same clarions that blared during drills, yet they sounded different this time, as if there was a little extra distress to them.

"We'd better get inside," he said.

Millard was already heading for the door of his workshop. Terry started to follow, then realized that Millard's double was frozen in place.

"Come along…what's your name?"

"Mill," the twin said absently.

Mill and Millard, Terry thought. That works.

"What is that noise?" Mill demanded. It sounded like a hundred bugles blowing.

"Power failure," Millard said. "I thought that might happen."

"From your experiment?" Terry asked. It was just like his best friend to put everyone in danger. Spell Realm's terraforming was still hundreds of years from being finished. A person could survive outside the containment field for a few minutes, which was an improvement over the instant freezing that would have happened fifty-three years ago.

"Nothing permanent," Millard said, opening the door to the workshop and ushering them in. "But it probably means I won't be able to replicate the experiment any time soon."

"Experiment?" Mill repeated, as if it was a word he'd never heard before. "Is that like a spell?"

Millard laughed. "I never thought of it that way before, but in a way it might be seen as a spell. We call it science."

Terry looked from one to the other. Except for their clothing, they looked exactly alike, even down to the way they wore their hair.

And neither seemed as frightened as they should be.

"I'm glad both of you are so intrigued," Terry muttered. "But if Mr. Jolley finds out what you've done, Millard, he'll take away your toys."

Mr. Jolley was in charge of Spell Realm's infrastructure and technically Millard and Terry's boss. Jolley had tried to get Millard under control but had eventually thrown up his hands and given up. But because Terry and Millard were friends, Terry got the brunt of the frustration this caused.

"Mr. Jolley's off-planet for the week," Millard said. "That's why I timed the experiment for today."

"Are you saying your Spell of Protection failed?" Mill asked sharply, looking alarmed for the first time.

"A Spell of Protection?" Millard laughed, then looked thoughtful. "Yes, that would be accurate enough."

"I must return to my own world immediately," Mill said. "My master, Lumbli, is in the capital. He left me in charge of protecting the realm." He went to the door but was frustrated by the latch. Terry caught up to him before he could figure it out, putting his hand on the twin's arm, intending to coax him away from the door.

Mill whirled around and pushed Terry backward. Terry stumbled, mostly from surprise. "Unhand me, cur!" Mill said.

Terry's hip slammed against the workbench, and he groaned. How many times had he wanted to wring Millard's neck? Well, here was his chance. This "Mill" didn't even officially exist. No one would miss him.

Millard laughed. "Cur? Oh, he's got your number, Terry. Tell me, Mill. Who is Terry in your world?"

"Teric is chief stableboy, under the Master of the Horses, Luncier."

"That sounds about right," Millard said, turning to Terry with his eyebrows raised.

Stableboy? And yet, Terry wasn't completely insulted. In fact, he'd used this very same description of his duties in a letter home to his parents. "Very funny," he said. "But this place wouldn't last long without me. I wonder if you don't underestimate the me of your world—this Teric—just as much."

Mill gave him an uncomprehending look.

Millard gestured for his double to sit down. "It won't do you any good to go outside…Mill. It won't get you home any faster. We'll just have to wait. They'll have the containment shield repaired soon, just as I'm certain your Spell of Protection is being fixed right now."

Mill hesitated, then sat down, wrapping his red robes around him with as much dignity as he could muster.

"I have a question for you," Millard said. "At the moment of transition, what exactly were *you* up to, Mill?"

Mill looked away, his cheeks turning red. "I was trying to capture the Majestic Ultima."

"What's that?" Terry asked.

"The common folk call it a unicorn," Mill answered.

Terry could still hear alarms sounding in the distance. They probably weren't in real danger. There was enough atmosphere and warmth inside the inner containment fields to keep people safe long enough to evacuate, but staying here was an unnecessary risk. "Sounds to me like you're idiots in both worlds," Terry said.

Millard was undeterred. "And is that a *dangerous* spell?"

Again, Mill refused to meet his twin's eye.

"I thought so," Millard said. "I suspect that neither spell nor experiment would have worked without the other. Indeed, it may not be replicable, which means I will never be able to publish it." He looked regretful.

Mill threw up his hands, as Terry had seen Millard do a hundred times when he was frustrated. Then he lowered them slowly, as if a thought had occurred to him. "Perhaps not all is lost. Your Mr. Jolley. Is he a master wizard?"

Millard didn't laugh. "I suppose he is, in a way. For certain, I have no other master."

"Lumbli won't stop searching for me. Perhaps, if your master is willing to help, we can make the magic once again happen at the same moment."

"Synchronicity doesn't seem out of the question to me," Millard said. "But until we can bring your Master Lumbli and my Mr. Jolley together, there is not much we can do, is there?"

"Master Lumbli won't be happy," Mill said.

Millard squirmed as little in his seat. "Neither will my boss. But they can't deny the brilliance of what we've done, can they?"

Mill brightened up. "That is certainly true." They grinned at each other at exactly the same moment in exactly the same way, perfect mirror images. Terry couldn't repress a shudder.

"Meanwhile," Millard said, "I postulate that our two worlds must be very similar for you to be here. I wonder if we have arrived at the same place using different terminology."

"Indeed," Mill said. "Though I believe my being able to

cross over to here means that my magic is stronger than your science."

"I would submit that the opposite is true," Millard said. "After all, you were drawn here, while I have remained in my own world."

They started arguing. Millard used scientific terms Terry was only vaguely familiar with, while Mill was using arcane terms he'd *never* heard—at least, most of them. Occasionally they stumbled across a word with the same meaning, and it delighted them both. *Quantum.* The word appeared to represent poorly misunderstood magic in both worlds. Soon they were talking so rapidly that Terry couldn't even make out the individual words, and he thought, *I might as well be invisible and deaf.*

In the distance, the alarms shut off one by one, until only the sound of Mill and Millard arguing filled the air.

This must be what it's like to be in Millard's head, Terry thought, and shuddered again.

The door to the shed flew open and Shara entered, her hair windswept, her cheeks red from the cold. She stopped dead in her tracks, looking from Mill to Millard and from Millard to Mill.

Mill scrambled to his feet and bowed deeply. "Lady Sharina," he said in an awed voice. "I am honored."

"Oh, Millard," Shara said, her voice dropping an octave. "What have you done now?"

Chapter 7

I worry that without me, Halor will be alone. He is famous and knows many people, but he has no true friends. He can talk shop with Carl Lundy, but only at the most basic, mechanistic levels. Those scientists who might be his equal have proven to be unreliable, trying to pry secrets from my husband, which offends him.

Our daughter, Shara, is much like him; too smart for her own good. Halor tells me that she is most like me, but I see both of us in her, and also another person altogether. She will make her own way, I can see that already, no matter what guidance we give her. I have seen her reject all advice and be proven right by dint of sheer willpower.

Halor sees me as an equal despite my lack of scientific prowess. I have skills he'd never even thought about before meeting me. He watches me with a smile on his face as I deal with businesspeople and scammers, bankers and frauds, captains of industry and delivery drivers.

Halor will continue on without me, doing what he's always done. But innovation in Spell Realm will come to an end, despite all his tinkering. Flexstone was the kind of game-changing technology that only comes along once a generation, and even Halor Mansing will have a hard time topping it.

— Martinique Mansing

Shara was manning the information booth when the power went out, so when she scurried off, it was, in effect, a dereliction of duty. But she wasn't worried about the guests. All their costumes were equipped with safety features, and most of the creatures and digital effects in the park had their own power source. It was only the larger structures that were still susceptible to a power grid failure.

She knew immediately that it was her stepbrother's doing. Millard had been hinting for days about a big experiment, one that would change the world. She didn't doubt it. She'd known from the first time she'd met him that Millard wasn't just a genius, he had the kind of intellect that would change mankind's fortunes—for better or worse.

Shara had always been at the top of her class. Only her doctorate remained, which was little more than a formality. But Millard, who was two years younger than her, was as advanced beyond her as she was beyond her classmates. She knew that one of these days, he was going to do something astounding.

"Will you handle the desk for a while?" she asked the new girl—*Keniss, I think?*

"Me?" Keniss appeared completely flabbergasted. She hadn't even handled routine duties yet, and here she was being asked to take over in an emergency.

"Thanks," Shara said and hurried away before the flustered girl could object.

Millard's workshop was on the border of the real world, and she doubted very much that he was wearing a costume of any kind. Shara couldn't be sure that he would look up long enough from his work to notice the danger.

As she hurried out the back door of Castle La Magie and into the work zone beyond, she shivered in the sudden cold, and she hadn't gone ten paces before she was gasping for breath. For all her concern about Millard, she'd forgotten to wear a costume herself. But she'd be fine as long as she didn't tarry too long.

To her relief, Millard was already inside his workshop, along with Terry, as usual. The older boy flushed at her entrance and averted his eyes. He wouldn't be able to get three words out now that she was there. It didn't matter what Shara tried to do to make him relax, Terry was completely intimidated by her. Why, she couldn't fathom. Sometimes, if they were alone long enough, she could get him to actually carry on a conversation, but that seemed to happen less and less.

She thought he'd delayed going back to school because of her, but then, he hadn't done a single thing to act on his feelings, despite her doing everything she could to signal that she was interested.

Maybe I shouldn't be, she thought. *Maybe he's just a lunk.*

But then, those brief conversations had been fun and interesting and genuine. There was a real man behind the awkward boyish stammering.

She turned to Millard…and to Millard.

It wasn't a digital effect, she was certain. Both Millards were clutching coffee cups, the same coffee cups that Shara had drunk out of a hundred times. If this doppelgänger was a flex-creature, it was the best she'd ever seen. While all the creatures and many of the attractions of Spell Realm were flex-creatures, they'd realized in the first year that they wouldn't be able to use them as human reproductions. No matter how advanced the technology, the uncanny valley effect always interfered with the results. In fact, the closer the flex-creatures had gotten to real humans, the more creeped out the guests had been.

It was the biggest expense in the park, having to hire flesh and blood humans to be the fair maids and villains and background color—fortunately for generations of college students needing to earn money during the summer.

But this *had* to be a flex-creature. What else could it be?

He was wearing red robes but was otherwise identical to her brother. Other-Millard rose to his feet and bowed. "Lady Sharina," he said, his voice hushed. "I am honored."

And then she knew. This was a real person. And Millard had invaded another reality, despite all the warnings not to.

"Oh, Millard…what have you done?"

But her stepbrother wasn't in the slightest bit chagrined. He was laughing. "Lady!" he said, unable to restrain his glee. "He sure has you figured out, sister o'mine."

Shara glanced at Terry, who was unable to hold back a grin. She frowned at him, but still he smiled.

It was a sore point for her, no matter how many times Millard needled her about being a "princess." No matter how many times her father asked her to wear the flowing gowns of park royalty, she'd always refused. She wore a scullery maid's costume more often than not.

She couldn't help who her father was, any more than Millard could. He was one to talk, the privileged little runt.

"Dad's going to ground you for life," she said.

Millard shrugged. "Right up until the moment he asks how the hell I did it."

He was right, of course. The news of this achievement would quickly spread, unless...

"Are you sure you want everyone to know?" Terry asked, finishing her thought. "I mean, this will change everything. Who knows how long it will be before you are left alone long enough to do it again? If ever."

Millard was staring at her, as if he'd already figured it out. "I guess it's up to my sister," he said.

"Your sister?" the duplicate Millard asked.

Shara turned to him and extended her hand. He stared at it for a moment and then limply put out his own hand, as if he'd never shaken hands before.

"My name is Shara, by the way," she said, "not Sharina."

"Lady Sharina," Millard hooted.

"My name is Mill," he said. "I'm sorry to have greeted you wrongly. In my world, you are the Lady Sharina, a royal princess, heir to the throne. I have seen you only from afar, for I am a commoner, raised up by my magic skills, to be sure, but still of common blood."

"Well, in this world, we don't pay any attention to such nonsense as 'common blood,'" Shara said, feeling offended on behalf of this new Mill. He was much more polite than her brother, so looks weren't everything.

"So, are you going to tell on me?" Millard asked.

"Not if you behave yourself. I'm sure that...Mill...would like to go home." She looked to him for confirmation, and he hesitated before nodding. "So, your name is Mill, and my double is named Sharina, and..." She motioned toward Terry, who said, "Apparently I have a twin named Teric."

"And yet," Shara continued, "in your world, you don't *know* my double. So the parallels aren't exact."

"But they are amazingly close to what I predicted," Mill said. It surprised her. It sounded like something a scientist would say, not a magician. She stared at him for a long moment.

Then an image of poor Keniss at the information booth being besieged by guests entered her mind, and she felt a twinge of guilt. "Terry, would you mind coming outside with me for a moment? I have something to ask of you."

He looked surprised, but gulped and nodded.

She turned at the door. "And you…" She pointed at Millard, then Mill, and then back again. "Both of you. It would be best if you don't both show your faces in public at the same time."

As Terry followed her out the door, Shara heard Millard—at least, she thought it was Millard—saying, "We must write down as many parallels and divergences as we can think of."

The door slammed, and they were outside. It was still a little chilly, but the air was rich with oxygen again, and Shara took a deep breath and started walking toward Castle La Magie, which was once again brightly lit.

"How are you, Terry?"

He shrugged. "Nothing Millard does surprises me anymore. It just is what it is, you know? I mean, he's barely gotten started, and look what he's done!"

"That's what concerns me," she said.

"I realize you're always worried about him," he ventured.

"No, it's more than that. Don't you realize what's happened?"

"Uh, maybe I don't understand it all."

"There are two of them! Two arrogant little geniuses who have no boundaries, who no doubt are even now hatching plans. If it doesn't scare you, Terry, it should."

He didn't reply, and she wondered if raising her voice had forever silenced him. But then he nodded. "I see your point, Shara. That is concerning."

"You'll need to keep an eye on them. Call in sick. I'm sure Mr. Lundy will let you have a few days off. Make sure Mill and Millard don't start anything. I'll get out of my duties and join you as soon as I can."

"All right, but…" Terry ventured, then stopped.

"But what?" she prompted.

"Do you really think we can stop Millard from doing what he wants?"

She laughed grimly. "Oh, he'll obey me, if I have to tie him down."

Terry laughed, a full-throated belly laugh. It was a surprisingly nice laugh. Shara reached out and put her hand on his shoulder. "Terry, my man, you can't afford to be shy with me anymore. We're partners now. You call me if anything happens. Right away. Don't hesitate, you hear?"

He nodded.

"You understand, Terry?" she repeated.

"Yeah," he said, and it seemed to Shara as if a weight lifted off his shoulders. He even laughed again. "I'm glad you came, Shara. I wasn't sure what to do."

She smiled. "Me either. I just know that we've got a couple of genius teenagers on our hands. Grounding isn't going to be enough. You head on back; I'll spell you tomorrow. One of us needs to be with them at all times."

He smiled and put out his hand. "Partners."

She ignored his outstretched hand and gave him a tight hug instead, then walked away without looking back.

Chapter 8

When I first met Halor, he had little regard for his own health or safety. He lived alone in a dormitory room because no roommate could put up with his eccentricities for long. But as soon as we married and had a child, he changed. He was determined to spend ample time with me and Shara in addition to pursuing his work, which had put him well on the way to becoming the richest man in history.

I insisted that he take time off, that he indulge in the occasional vacation. And one day a week is set aside for Shara and me, no matter how busy he is.

I can still make him laugh. I can see him relax when Shara is with him.

I worry what will happen when I'm gone. I worry that he will lose his sense of humor. But most of all, I worry that he will neglect Shara's true needs in his obsessive need to protect and care for her.

— Martinique Mansing

When Terry was certain that the two geniuses wouldn't start another experiment or spell anytime soon, he slipped away. The pair didn't appear to notice him leaving; they were too deep into their analysis of their mutual triumph.

Terry turned on his phone and, sure enough, there was a string of messages from Carl Lundy. His boss had ordered him to turn off his phone when off-duty, freely admitting that he might be called in at any time otherwise. At first Terry had thought he was kidding, but after having several free days interrupted in a row, he'd started turning it off.

"Don't be an easy mark," his boss had said. "People will take advantage of you."

But this was different. Terry had known the moment the lights blinked off that Carl would need him. Power grids didn't handle sudden overloads and shutoffs well; if there were any weaknesses in the system, they tended to show up when high demands were put on them.

"Thank you for answering, Terrance," his boss said. "You know I hate to bother you, but we have a bit of situation here. Can you come to the main power plant right away?"

"Yes, sir," Terry said. Shara had told him to stay with Mill and Millard, but the worst of the damage had already been done. His sense of duty warred with his promise, but routine was too hard to break. "I'll be right there."

"Good man," Carl said. "And by the way, you wouldn't know what caused, this by any chance? Have you seen Millard lately?"

"I spent the afternoon with him, sir. He's...he's with a good friend from off-world."

"Hmmm. All right, Terry, if you say so. But I'd appreciate a warning next time." He clicked off before Terry had to lie again.

The power plant was humming and grinding and then humming again, and Carl's face was lighting up and glowering and lighting up in response. Terry was surprised to see Maxwell Carnigan there, his scrawny arms and legs barely animating his overalls. He moved as if he was gliding across the floor. Mr. Carnigan had been Carl's boss a long time ago and was still called in on emergencies.

"Everything has blown a gasket, kiddo," Mr. Carnigan muttered when he saw Terry.

"A gasket, sir?" *I'm not going to ask what "kiddo" means.*

"An old Earth term. Meaning everything is kaput, dead, useless."

"We'll fix it, Mr. Carnigan. We have plenty of backup parts."

"Till the next time," the old man muttered darkly. "And the next."

Terry dove into the repairs, happy to be working for a couple of reasons. First of all, he loved getting grease on his hands. Most people never saw the machinery behind the miracles of everyday life, especially in the park. But no matter how sophisticated and how miniaturized it all became, it still came down to moving parts; gears and oil and belts. Terry felt as if he was Dorothy from the old Earth story and he was seeing behind the Wizard of Oz's curtain.

But the second reason was even stronger than the first. It took his mind off of Shara and her hug, and her telling him to quit being bashful. It was embarrassing, all the more so for being true. When he had first met her, he'd been sure that she was a digital illusion, a costume, but she was real—and funny and thoughtful, and they'd eventually had a great conversation.

He'd turned off his costume early on, watching her carefully to catch her reaction. She hadn't blinked an eye, though his Personage was taller, darker, and handsomer than he was. She was wearing a new model of princess, one he hadn't seen before. Instead of blonde, she was raven-haired, with her hair cut short. Her eyes were dark brown and slightly slanted upward, and she had high cheekbones and an oval face. He was in love with the Personage, but even more enamored with the person behind it.

Finally, he'd asked, "What Personage are you wearing? I don't think I've ever seen it before. It's very attractive."

She'd flushed, and he had immediately understood his mistake. "This is all me," she'd managed to say.

From then on, their easy camaraderie had disappeared. Why couldn't she have been average looking, even unattractive? She was way out of his league, the kind of woman who didn't give grease monkeys like him the time of day.

The three generations of grease monkeys quickly replaced the blown "gaskets," mostly old parts that would have needed to be replaced during the next routine servicing anyway. Terry glanced up once and saw the contented looks on Carl and old Maxwell's faces and knew that he had the same expression.

Let Millard be the genius inventor; Terry was content with fixing things.

A few years after Shara's mother had died, Halor Mansing had gone off-world for several months. The bride he'd returned with was not, as everyone expected, a young woman of childbearing years, but a woman his own age with a young son. There'd been some friction at first between Millard and Shara, but eventually they'd settled into a comfortable big sister/little brother rivalry.

The machines stopped grinding and only hummed, and Carl pronounced himself satisfied. "Thank you for coming in on your day off, Terry."

"I was happy to. Besides, this was an emergency. I think that's in the contract."

"You have a contract?" Carl asked, sounding shocked. He turned to Maxwell. "You never gave me a contract."

"I gave you the back of my hand, that's what I did. Contracts ain't worth the pads they're printed on."

"You know what I mean," Terry said lamely.

"I do indeed, and I thank you again," Carl said. "But I have another favor to ask. Would you bring Millard Mansing around tomorrow? I'd like to have a word with him."

"Sir," Terry said, "he didn't mean to cause an outage."

"No?" Carl said. "Well, I don't think he *did* cause it. Oh, I noticed the power surge this afternoon, but it was well within limits. That is, if the system hadn't already been stressed."

"Stressed?" Terry said. "What was stressing it?"

"Damned if I can figure it out. That's why I want to talk to our resident boy genius. It's got something to do with a burst of Fanchon Particles, that's all I know."

"I'll see if he can come," Terry said.

"Please do." Carl sounded worried. "I don't like what happened today. From what I can tell, the Fanchon Particles are increasing exponentially."

"What?" Maxwell said. He'd been ignoring them, going around the machinery and rubbing and tapping things. Now he turned and frowned. "Exponential is never good."

"Yeah, well our system can handle it, I think," Carl said. "But I'd like to make sure."

"I'll bring him by first thing in the morning," Terry promised.

And if Millard balks, I'll put Mill into overalls and let him do his magic.

He smiled as he walked away.

Chapter 9

I have resisted the immense pressure to franchise Spell Realm.

For one thing, I know that it would put Halor in an early grave. No matter how many times he might be told that he is not responsible for the franchises, he would take each and every one of them under his supervision.

There is also the problem of keeping control of our patents. It's difficult to reverse engineer Flexstone when it's only used for construction, because we have been able to keep strict control. We can't be so sure about other applications. So, except for in the park itself, Flexstone has only been allowed for building purposes.

And finally, I have my father's experience to remember. He was a successful small businessman who expanded, continued his success, and expanded again and again until one day he was in over his head and the whole enterprise fell apart.

Businesses will expand to their level of incompetence.

My father needed a keeper, which my mother was ill-suited to be. I have taken this role with Halor and drilled into him the dangers of expansion. I hope it will be enough.

Besides, what is the need? The money is already coming in so fast we can't spend it all!

— Martinique Mansing

Mill was surprised by how quickly he accepted that he was in a new world. The clincher for him was how different Shara—this world's Lady Sharina—was from his own.

Mill had loved Lady Sharina from afar for all his life. He had never spoken to her, and as far as he knew, she had never even glanced his way. He'd been in the same ballroom with her, along with hundreds of other people. Once, she had beckoned Lumbli to her side and Mill had started to follow, but his master had waved him away from behind his back. Later, Lumbli hadn't even bothered to tell Mill what the summons was about.

To see Lady Sharina, or someone who looked and acted just like her, from only inches away had been more than he could have ever hoped for. She'd even spoken to him!

Oh, she was dressed like a commoner, and her hair was short, but Mill had already figured out that that was the affectation in this world. That there were still class distinctions, he had no doubt. She had subtly talked down to this reality's Teric, though they'd pretended to be equals. Or perhaps that had been because of the gulf in intelligence between them.

Is Lady Sharina intelligent? Mill had never thought to even ask it, and if he had, it wouldn't have mattered. But perhaps merit mattered in this reality, in which case, he should have no trouble fitting in.

Already, in talking to his double, he'd realized that the science of this world was simply a different manifestation of the magic in his world.

He watched Lady Shara leave with Terry, amazed at their familiarity. He wanted to trail along silently, just to listen to her voice, but she was probably making plans, giving Terry orders.

"I think, terminology aside, that you and I are talking about the same processes," Millard said, breaking through his thoughts.

"Yes, but you must use mechanical means to reach the same ends," Mill said, feeling vaguely superior because of it.

Millard waved that off. "No doubt there are a few differences in the physics of your reality, but they must be very close. I believe if you and I can align our two methods, we might be able to create a permanent wormhole."

Wormhole? Mill smiled, thinking of a worm's path through an apple. It was strangely appropriate. "I'm not so sure," he answered. "While the apple might be the same, the tree would be separate, and the ground beneath. A wind, a rainstorm, and the apple might fall, and who knows what the consequences would be?"

"We'd have to find a way to anchor it," Millard agreed. "But I'll bet you the two of us can figure that out."

Mill smiled. It was like talking to himself, only better, as if he'd experienced two different lives, both of which he could bring to spellcasting. Together, they might be twice as powerful, or as, sometimes happened with spells when two wizards were involved, the effect might even be stronger.

"The synergies are interesting to contemplate," Millard said, as if reading his mind—which, in a way, he was. Even without asking for the definition of "synergy," Mill thought he knew what it meant.

Neither of them asked the question of whether they should attempt such a thing. It passed briefly through Mill's mind, but the image of Lady Shara (as he had decided to call her) removed all doubts. He'd stay and learn what he could.

"Good," Millard said. "We'll start fresh in the morning. But for now, I'm famished. A good night's sleep would help too." He got up and walked toward the door.

"What about me?" Mill asked.

Millard turned, looking confused. Mill realized he was being given a glimpse of his own behavior. How many times had Lumbli called him a "thoughtless boy"?

"I have a cot," Millard said, looking around the workshop. "Somewhere."

He dug around in the pile of machines along the wall and pulled out a rickety contraption that unfolded into something that looked like narrow bed.

"There you are," Millard said.

"I'm hungry too, Millard." *Surely, I'm not* this *thoughtless!*

"Oh, of course. I'll send someone with a meal. No...I'd better come myself. Best not to confuse people."

Mill laughed, and after a few moments, Millard joined him. "Sorry, it's like I've been talking into a mirror. I forget you are another person."

Mill nodded. "If your Mr. Jolley is anything like my Master

Lumbli, we'd best keep this to ourselves if we want to be left alone to do our spells."

"Agreed," Millard said, but then stood there as if at a loss.

"Perhaps," Mill ventured, "you should ask Lady Shara. She'll know what to do. And perhaps she can bring some food and some blankets?"

"Shara?" Millard considered this. "Maybe so, but she'd never let me forget it."

He seemed to have figured out a solution, because he turned to leave again. Mill wasn't so sure that his double wouldn't forget him the minute he left the workshop.

"Millard?" he called after him. "I have an idea, if you're willing."

Chapter 10

I have tried to make Spell Realm affordable for everyone. But, of course, even traveling here from off-planet is far beyond the means of most people. Most of our visitors are wealthy, so we must cater to them, with fine dining, personal tours, and ready access to the popular attractions.

But it is possible to wander through Spell Realm, not spend any money at all, and still experience the fantasy. Indeed, many of our employees, who have their travel expenses to Spell Realm paid and who also are given free food and lodging, manage to save most of their wages and still enjoy themselves in their off hours.

I have strict rules of conduct while they are at work, but what they do when they aren't working isn't any of my business. I'm sure many of them get into mischief, bless them.

— Martinique Mansing

An hour later, dressed in Millard's overalls, Mill ventured into Castle La Magie. Millard had assured him he'd be in his own quarters by then, so there'd be no chance of them being in the same place at the same time.

Mill watched the expressions of passersby for any sign of recognition, but most of them ignored him. Apparently, they were "tourists," which he gathered was some type of nobility who traveled about for fun. He'd heard of such things on his world, but most never came to his part of the woods.

But some things were the same. Mill was dressed as a worker, so he was barely worth noticing. As he entered the back door of the castle, he heard the clattering of dishes and headed that way. A vestibule was to one side, and someone hissed at him from it. He looked over to see a cadaverous man waving him over.

"Good tidings," Mill said.

"Don't even try to pretend, Millard," the man said rudely. "You're hopeless at it. But the least you could do is wear your Personage when you're in the park."

Millard had warned him that the overalls would be frowned upon but had assured him no one would say anything. "It…" He struggled to remember the word his double had used to describe the failure of the spell. "…malfunctioned."

"Really? And you couldn't fix it? How odd. Well, it's not like I can do anything about it, you being the favored son."

So Millard was royalty here, and yet this commoner was questioning him. "Shall we go have a talk with my father now? Perhaps you can tell him about my faults."

The man turned gratifyingly pale. "I'm just trying to help."

Mill didn't bother to answer, just strode into the dining hall. He looked around for a private table. He found one in the shadows of one corner and had barely sat down before a young woman dressed in a gown shorter than any he'd ever seen approached with a wide smile. He tried to look into her eyes, not stare at her legs.

"Millard!" she said, sounding delighted. "You so rarely take a table!"

"Yes, well…it has been an exceedingly long day. The… malfunction…"

"We had to serve people using candles!" the woman said. "It was rather romantic." She winked at him. "It made me think of you."

Mill was astounded. He'd heard of women in the cities who were so forward. Apparently, you could pay them for the pleasure of their company. He'd never expected it to be so blatant.

Someone from three tables over spoke up. "Could you get me a refill, Kirrie?"

She shouted over her shoulder, "Hold your horses!" then leaned down and said, "I'm off in an hour. You want to come to my room?"

Mill nodded, unable to speak. If he was going to explore this world, he needed to learn its ways fast. Besides, if this woman was offering what he thought she was offering, it beat sleeping on a cot.

"Good," she said. "I'll be back with your favorite meal in a jiffy."

Mill looked around the room, dazed. No one had paid any attention to their planned liaison, and he had a feeling that if anyone had, they wouldn't have cared. He'd thought this world would be similar to his, and in many ways it was, but there was one very big difference: the people.

His favorite meal appeared to be some kind of meat, ground up and squeezed into a flat circle, with sauces and pickled vegetables on top, set between two thick pieces of bread. He took one bite and restrained a groan of pleasure.

He was going to like this new world.

Chapter 11

A man's home is his castle.

In the case of Halor Mansing and his lady, this is literally true. Even if we wanted to live humbly, our fame is such that it wouldn't be safe. To keep some measure of privacy, we have taken the tallest tower of Castle La Magie as our residence.

As straightforward as I wish we could be, we've also had to make the entrances to these accommodations somewhat secret and hard to find, with only a few of our upper management knowing how to reach us.

We have become lord and lady of the manor despite our wishes.

I realized, after a time, that to enforce our authority, perhaps one king should be allowed. A Personage was created for Halor, a magnificent illusion that to me only expresses his inner nobility. I have seen him wear this Personage only once, during the grand opening. Mostly, he walks among the gaily costumed visitors in a suit and tie, which sets him apart as much as a crown.

For my part, I play the lady, for it makes it easier to give orders. This isn't a comfortable persona, but it is a necessary one. I hope someday to become just another old lady, indistinguishable from the elders who vacation here.

— Martinique Mansing

As Millard made his way to his rooms through the crowds, he was unaware of the whispers. He never wore a Personage, though it might have disguised him. His picture had been plastered throughout the inhabited worlds, the unexpected prince of Spell Realm. His mother's wedding to Halor Mansing had been front-page news for months. But Millard had spent most of that time in his workshop, working on his new idea.

His room was on a private corridor, at the end of which was a large portrait of the mistress of Spell Realm. But it was not his mother. Instead, he confronted Martinique Mansing's intimidating and penetrating gaze, which seemed to fix upon him the moment the elevator doors opened. She was round faced, almost plump. Her neck was a little too thick to be that of a classical beauty. Millard had a feeling that she had insisted on a realistic likeness, that nothing be hidden.

But it was her eyes that caught him. She had deep brown eyes, almost soft, and yet they seemed to look right through him. He usually averted his gaze, but today he looked up into her implacable expression and stuck his tongue out.

She winked.

He stopped dead in his tracks, unable to move. A cold chill went down his spine. He stared at the portrait, trying to figure out how he'd imagined such a thing.

She winked again.

Millard cried out and started to turn, ready to run back to the elevator, but then something else caught his eye. There was another person in the huge picture. He'd never really examined the landscape before. Castle La Magie was in the background. In the foreground, there were large trees, which he recognized as the Mossy Forest. But he'd never noticed that poking her head around one of the tree trunks was a red-haired woman. Her hair was a frizzy halo, and even from a distance, he could make out the freckles on her pale face.

She waved to him.

He groaned and closed his eyes. This was impossible. His mother was dead, he was sure of it. First the unicorn, then his other self, and now this. It was all connected, he was sure. The door he'd opened wasn't completely closed.

He opened his eyes and forced himself to look at the picture.

It was back to normal. Martinique Mansing stared down at him judgmentally again, without the teasing wink. He shook it off and forced himself to walk the last ten steps to his door.

He reached out, in his mind already turning the knob, and

the door opened as if his fingers were upon it. He didn't freeze this time, but pushed the door the rest of the way open, went inside, and slammed it behind him.

Millard stood leaning with his back to the door, breathing heavily. He was safe. He wasn't sure how he knew, but his room was still his room. There was nothing "other" about it.

It was his own willpower that made it so, he realized deep within. Just as it was his willpower that had opened the door. Just as it was his desire to meet Martinique Mansing and to see his own mother again that had animated the portrait.

It wasn't until he'd arrived at Spell Realm that he had realized that Martinique was almost as famous as her husband, at least among those who didn't care about science. It was she who'd made something of the invention of Flexstone, and she who controlled what happened to it. She was widely regarded as the world builder, the force behind Spell Realm.

Among those who wanted the secret of Flexstone, she was known as the Witch of Spell Realm, for she wouldn't allow the invention to be used for anything but the most basic of building blocks. Even that had changed the economy of the inhabited worlds. It was cheap and effective, and anyone could afford it and use it, even in the harshest of climates. Spell Realm collected a small percentage from each brick, and so many were sold that it was enough to create a new world, a world of fantasy, the world of Martinique Mansing's imagination.

And then she'd died, a freak accident, somehow straying past the safety zone and falling into one of the deep crevasses that surrounded Spell Realm.

Millard flopped onto his bed, trying not to think about what happened next.

If outworlders had thought that Martinique's death would free Halor Mansing to use Flexstone for greater use, they were mistaken. Halor had retreated to his castle, rarely to emerge. Spell Realm continued on as before, but the world building stopped. Everything was maintained as the Witch of Spell Realm had left it.

It had been surprising to everyone, therefore, when Halor Mansing had left Spell Realm for a short time, visiting an obscure planet and coming back with a new bride and a genius stepson.

That had been a glorious few years. Millard could remember it only as a blur. He'd enjoyed every part of Spell Realm, taken every tour, and wandered around on his own after that. His mother, to his surprise, had been devoted to her new husband, doting over him. She gained weight, which bothered her, and took to wearing her Personage of a slender queen everywhere but in her private chambers.

Halor Mansing, for his part, had seemed content.

And then, as usual, his mother had gone and ruined it. She'd run off with a delivery boy, the captain of a small supply ship, and they had been so eager to get away that they had plastered themselves into the side of an asteroid. There'd been nothing left but bits and pieces of metal.

For a long time, Millard harbored the illusion that his mother would return, repentant. She'd always been a flake; she wasn't really even certain who Millard's father was, as he discovered after hearing ten different stories about him.

But she was really gone.

Strangely, it hadn't hurt Spell Realm. If anything, Halor Mansing had become even more famous. It sometimes seemed as if half the women who arrived at the park wanted to meet the notorious inventor and to mother the young boy whose own mother had abandoned him.

Millard had retreated to his laboratory, and Halor Mansing had retreated to his tower, and the only conduit between them for a long time had been his stepsister, Shara. It was only in the last few months that either of them had begun to emerge from their shell.

Well, he'd broken out, all right. In fact, now there were two of him!

It was ironic to look into his other self's eyes and envy the magic he saw there, and even more ironic that his other self obviously envied him his knowledge of science.

He drifted off to sleep thinking of unicorns and dragons.

"Mill."

Millard opened his eyes. Only his mother called him Mill, but this was a man's voice.

Looming over him was a tall figure with dark eyes, darker than the room. Millard tried to cry out, to roll off the bed, but he couldn't move. The sound in his throat was strangled. The man looked a little like Carl Lundy, but taller, skeletal, and bald.

"What have you done now, Mill?" the figure asked.

And then Millard woke up, the sun shining in his eyes. He breathed deeply, trying to regain his calm. He rose and went to the window. The light was strange, as if muted by haze. The sunlight was never obscured in Spell Realm; at least, not as long as Millard had been there.

There were no clouds, and yet something was occluding the light, as if it was passing through a screen. He shook his head and went back to bed, intending to close his eyes and block it out.

Something's gone wrong, came the thought, and nothing could dispel it.

Chapter 12

Before I met Halor, I never questioned the nature of reality. But as Spell Realm's illusions become more and more realistic, I have realized that "reality" is simply an agreed-upon story. And as a story, it can be changed, rewritten, in whole or in part. It is really up to the creator of the story, and no creator will create the exact same reality.

If the secret of Flexstone was to ever escape Spell Realm, I have no doubt that a thousand different storytellers would quickly create a thousand different realities. Flexstone can be used to represent anything the imagination can conceive.

It is almost enough for me to wish that the secret would escape— someday. But not now. Spell Realm has so much more to do before that time comes, to be an example to others. To show that the reality we were given is not the reality we have to keep.

— Martinique Mansing

Caleb was surprised to find out that the extraction team was already in Spell Realm. He had been ordered to help them. It didn't matter that he'd explained that he had no experience with such things.

"You're our man in place," his boss told him. "Assist them anyway you can."

"Sir, they might figure out it's me that fingered her. I spent all day yesterday with her," he protested.

His boss was implacable. "You'll be leaving with the extraction team, so it hardly matters what they suspect. Just get it done."

"Yes, sir. Where do I meet them?"

"Don't worry. They'll find you."

Caleb ended the call with a sigh. Shara Mansing was a nice girl, despite her negative reaction to his approaches. *I'd reject someone coming on to me that hard, too.* He had a sudden image of her gagged and blindfolded, being carried over the shoulder of some mercenary.

He looked in the mirror. *Am I doing the right thing?* He ran his hand down the ever-present cowlick over his forehead, frowning.

I need a drink.

He headed down to the bar, or rather, the way it was configured, the tavern. The wenches (and wastrels, for that matter) serving the drinks made it clear that they were as available as the ale, but he resisted. Having been so forward with Shara had been his way of testing her, trying to get a reaction. It hadn't been comfortable, and it was not the way he comported himself in the real world.

The whole fantasy thing gave him the willies. He liked things that were real and solid. He liked knowing that whatever he looked at really was what it looked like. He'd always been an errand boy—his testing had proven that he was honest and could be relied on not to examine the contents of the packets he carried. He'd been a stickler for rules since he was a small boy; it was amazing to him that his mere honesty was enough to give him a full-time job with a title that far outreached his actual power.

Apparently, the testing was completely reliable, because he was having a hard time doing something that was so obviously illegal—worse, that could hurt someone.

Turn yourself in to Halor Mansing, the little rule-following voice in his mind said. *If anyone has the power to protect you, it's him.*

Caleb raised his finger to the bartender and ordered then quickly downed another drink.

As if there was any way to see the great man. The founder of Spell Realm rarely left his tower. Most employees wouldn't even admit he was in residence.

Confess to Shara?

He shook his head. He looked up to see the bartender smiling wryly. Apparently, customers having silent talks with themselves was nothing new.

Shara thinks you're a douchebag, pal. She'd probably turn heel at the very sight of you.

Besides, betraying my employers is yet another rule I'd be breaking. Dammit!

Someone climbed up onto the stool next to Caleb, but he was too deep into his misery to look over.

"Buy me a drink?" a chipper voice said.

He turned to see a young woman with a round face smiling up at him. Her hair was bright yellow, with ringlets hanging down over her forehead. Her blue eyes were shining even in the dimness of the tavern. She was barely tall enough to climb up on the stool and looked far too young be in a tavern. The bartender must have thought so too, because he held out his hand.

The woman smiled at him and produced a small gold chain purse, from which she brought out an ID that satisfied the bartender.

Caleb nodded to the man, and the woman ordered a sangria. He winced. The wine was far too sweet for him, but then—he gave the stranger another look—she probably thrived on the stuff. *Sweet is as sweet does.*

She saluted him with her wineglass and gulped down her sangria. She closed her eyes blissfully and smacked her lips. Then she presented the glass to the bartender.

"Whatever the lady wants," Caleb said. "Put it on my tab." After all, how much could such a small woman drink?

She took a sip of the second serving, then put the glass down and appraised Caleb, looking up and down his lanky body. "You're one tall drink of water," she said. She put out her hand, which his fingers alone completely enveloped. "My name is Marie."

He returned the appraisal. She didn't look like a pro, more like a tourist who was looking for a good time. Fair enough. That didn't break his code of honor.

"Caleb," he said.

"Come join me and my sisters at our table?"

Sisters? Oh, well. He would put the drinks on his expense account. Research, so to speak.

She climbed down off the stool. Caleb stood politely and realized that the top of the woman's head barely reached his chest. She wore a princess gown, but it looked like she'd taken off most of the ruffles. Her movements were unexpectedly cat-like, like a trained gymnast's.

She turned and, with a come-hither wave, started toward the darkened corner of the bar. He followed, more out of curiosity than desire. He didn't know when the extraction team would show up, so he had nothing better to do.

Marie's sisters were as small as she was, but with completely different styles. One had short black hair, dark, heavy make-up, and was dressed as a yeoman archer in green and brown cotton and a leather jerkin. The third was drab compared to her sisters, with lank brown hair and a frumpy servant's dress.

It wasn't until Caleb sat down and three pairs of bright blue eyes regarded him that he realized they were actually identical triplets.

"These are my sisters, Trina," Marie pointed to the dark one, "and Selene," the drab one. "Sisters, this is Mr. Caleb Chance."

Caleb had begun to pull out a chair for himself, but at this introduction, he hesitated and straightened up. Had he mentioned his last name?

"So, Mr. Chance," the drab one, Selene, said. "Where do we find Shara Mansing?"

As Calip passed Castle La Magie, the first moon had risen above the highest tower, while the second moon was peeking over the horizon. He caught a glimpse of himself in the reflection of a puddle. He'd cut his hair close to his scalp, tired of fighting the cowlick that made him look foolish.

Calip was the Chance Knight.

It was chance that he was driving his cart to market that sunny morning, chance that he was passing by the meadow where Queen Margana had chosen to picnic. He saw the black knights charge and the Queen's bodyguards fall one by one.

It was chance that he picked up the fallen lance in time to

dismount a charging knight. He hadn't quite finished lifting the lance, and its base lodged firmly in the earth, and the knight rolled backward off his mount. It was chance that the sword he snatched from the ground found one of the weak spots in the second knight's armor. It was chance that the third black knight was thrown by his mount and landed on his head. And it was chance that help arrived in time to keep Calip from being skewered by the last of the enemy knights.

Calip had tried to get back to his cart, afraid that the perishable fruits had been too long in the sun. But a huge knight with golden armor had waylaid him and led him back to where Queen Margana was standing, looking around her in a daze. She came back to her senses when she saw him.

"You saved me, sir," she said in the breathless way she always spoke. "What is your name?"

"Calip, your majesty. But it was mere chance that anything I did helped. I am but a humble farmer."

"Mere chance?" she repeated, then laughed. "Then, Sir Chance, it was chance that saved me when all my honored knights failed. I trust in your chance, sir, for I intend for you to be knighted, and you shall serve me from this day forward."

Sometimes Calip, the Chance Knight, wished that day had never happened, though he was glad that Queen Margana was safe. She was a kind if absentminded mistress. Sometimes she looked at him as if she had forgotten who he was.

Calip was given a knight's rigorous training, but it was clear that he had no natural aptitude for fighting. So instead he became the queen's errand boy, doing all those things that the other knights wouldn't stoop to. He didn't mind. It gave him a chance to talk to people instead of just being ignored by the court nobility as beneath their notice.

When he was sent to spy on the small village at the base of Castle La Magie, he blended in easily with the farmers and merchants. His speech and manner reverted to that of his youth, and he felt himself relaxing.

Except when he thought of his mission.

It was still difficult to believe that Queen Margana wished to kidnap Lady Sharina. It was nothing but jealousy and envy.

The lady of Castle La Magie had caught the eye of young Duke Salern, who was the queen's lover. Instead of ignoring the dalliance, the queen had decided to take more drastic action.

At least she isn't asking me to kill *Lady Sharina.*

Yes, but what happens after she is taken?

Calip didn't want to think about that.

It hadn't taken him long to realize that Lady Sharina was unprotected. She was beloved by the townspeople and by the castle servants, so she was in no danger...or so she and her father believed. She often donned commoners' clothing to walk among her vassals incognito, or so she thought. The commoners played along, though their deference was obvious to anyone not to the manor born, someone like the Chance Knight.

Perhaps if I fail to report, Queen Margana will forget her peevishness.

And so the Chance Knight tarried, enjoying his sojourn among those born into his class. Who would have believed that simply blending in could be such a pleasure? He sat at the long bar of the Pronged Horse, staring at the famous painting of a unicorn by Leonardo. The only reason Castle La Magie existed, much less the village that surrounded it, was because of the unicorn that was occasionally sighted there. Because of that, lords and ladies from throughout the land visited the castle, and while Duke Mansing would never think to ask for payment for his accommodations, it was understood that a small gift was expected, and small gifts from nobility were enough to support the entire province.

Perhaps I'll go for a ride in the country tomorrow, Calip thought. *See if, as seems to so often happen, I will chance upon my desire.*

"Well met, Sir Chance. Buy me a drink?"

He knew before turning around that he needed to look down. Sister Marifor was a tiny woman, but deadly. He looked over her shoulder, and sure enough, the other two sisters, Trinafor (who glowered) and Selefor (who scowled) were sitting at a corner table.

"The queen sent *you*?" he said, unable to keep the dismay out of his voice. "I'd hoped that she would come to her senses."

"She is more determined than I have ever seen her," Marifor

said. She grinned as if she'd told a joke. "Determined" was not a word often used to describe the queen. "Though why she is interested in that fop Salern I'll never understand."

"What will you do after you've taken her?" There was no chance that Lady Sharina wouldn't recognize the Sister Executioners.

Marifor shrugged. "We have many clients, and we never tell. We'll let her go as soon as Queen Morgana and Duke Salern are betrothed."

"Wouldn't it be easier to dispose of Lady Sharina completely?"

Marifor's grin faltered slightly, and she looked away.

I'm finally running out of chances, he thought.

"So, Chance the Knight, where do we find Lady Sharina?"

Chapter 13

More than half of the Thousand Worlds were started by corporations, though many have lost control over time. There are a few worlds where the corporate culture is so strong that they continue to dominate the social structure.

We are one of those corporate worlds, but unlike any other. The windswept rocks and stormy oceans of the world the Spell Realm Corporation bought had few natural resources that anyone wanted.

We created the value of this world. It consists of the intangibles of pleasure and fantasy. It is bought and paid for by my husband's invention of Flexstone. It is the formula of this invention that everyone really wants. If not for that, we would be left alone to role-play to our hearts' content.

— Martinique Mansing

Terry awoke feeling vaguely guilty that he was late. Then he realized it was still dark outside. He wanted to be the one to roust Millard out of bed, but he had plenty of time. His friend rarely woke before midmorning.

He planned to take Millard directly to his boss, to make sure it got done. Otherwise, Millard would, without a doubt, ignore the message that Lundy wanted to talk to him. Besides, the longer he could keep Millard and Mill apart, the less trouble they could get into.

He let himself into the apartment. It was two rooms, twice as big as Terry's, and had a little kitchen alcove to boot, which Millard never used, of course. He had the kitchen staff make meals especially for him. Many of them fondly remembered when he was an irrepressible young boy, while the younger ones saw him as the hugely smart and not bad-looking, if short and usually disheveled, stepson of Spell Realm's owner. Something about him begged to be taken care of, and the kitchen staff was happy to oblige.

Millard was still in bed, fully clothed, his notepads and devices strewn about the covers. His workpad was pressed at an angle into his cheek, with drool running down the screen.

"Get up, you lazy bastard. You've got worlds to conquer," Terry said.

Millard groaned but sat straight up, the pad sticking to his cheek for a moment, then falling neatly into his hands. He looked down and started typing.

"Give it a rest, Millard," Terry said.

"I realized my mistake in the middle of the night," Millard replied. "I've got to run this by Mill."

"Get dressed and let's get something to eat first, all right?" Terry said.

"What are you," Millard grumbled, "my mother?"

Surprised, Terry didn't say anything. Millard rarely referred to his mother. Terry hadn't yet worked up the courage to ask Shara what had happened, and Mr. Mansing rarely left his offices on the top floors of Castle La Magie these days.

Millard disappeared into the bathroom for a few minutes, emerging in the same wrinkled clothing. "Let's go," he said. He seemed eager now, sweeping up the devices on the bed and secreting them in various pockets.

"You got your Personage?" Terry asked.

"I…I think I lost it," Millard said. He had been given, over his objections, a Personage of high noble status, a duke or a baron or something. He'd wanted a servant's garb so he could go about his business without all the scraping and bowing, both in the fantasy realm and in the real world.

"Well, I guess no one's going to give *you* a demerit, you lucky bastard."

For once, Millard looked abashed. "Sorry about that. I know it isn't fair, but these rules are too stupid to endure. Father will get around to admonishing me one of these days, and I'll act all contrite and obey the rules for a while, and then…" He shrugged as if to say, *Who cares?*

As they opened the door to leave, the lights flickered. Millard stopped dead in his tracks. He muttered, "I wonder if Mill…" then shook his head. "He can't be that quick a learner."

"That reminds me," Terry said, grabbing the opportunity. "Carl Lundy wants to talk to you."

Millard groaned. "Can't you just tell him it won't happen again?"

"He seems to think it wasn't your experiment that caused the power outage, or if it was, that it was only the last of a cascade. He wants to pick your brain."

That mollified Millard a little, though he still grumbled as they wandered down the hallway. Terry led the way to the staff dining room; otherwise, Millard was likely to miss his morning meal altogether—and his lunch—and maybe even his dinner, and then late in the evening, he'd wake the ever-patient kitchen staff to fix him something.

There was a long line at the buffet. Terry sighed and headed toward the end of the line. Millard kept walking toward the front. Terry didn't believe he meant to cut in—he was probably just deep in thought—but couldn't be sure. Millard wasn't above using his status to save him time he felt could be better used on something else.

"Wait your turn, Millard."

Millard turned, amazed that anyone should use such a tone with him. Granger loomed over him, pointing down at him with a bony finger. "You aren't real nobility, you know. You're a citizen, just like the rest of us. I don't care how rich your daddy is."

In a way, you had to admire Granger for his challenge. Most of the workers in Spell Realm let Millard have his way. Whether it was out of envy or a sense of fairness, Granger at least had the courage of his convictions.

"Oh, I wasn't going to–" Millard started to say, then Terry saw him getting angry. His eyes narrowed, and he thrust his chin forward like he did when he was ready for a fight. "I have important work I need to get to. What are your big plans,

Granger? Sucking up to fake princesses?"

Everyone froze and held their breath. Terry put out his hand to pull Millard away. "We can order a meal in the dining room," he began, when he felt something like a cold chill run through him, but instead of it striking his skin from the outside, it came from inside.

He didn't have his Personage turned on, but about half the workers did. Suddenly, everyone's real bodies were visible, most people wearing wrinkled, faded clothing, the women without makeup, the men unshaven.

Granger was naked.

Terry had always assumed that Granger was one of the park employees who chose to dress up in a real costume, over their real bodies, if for no other reason than he couldn't imagine anyone purposely choosing such a string-bean Personage.

But now a very short, very fat man stood there, looking down at himself in disbelief.

At that moment, the swinging doors to the kitchen opened and a young woman emerged carrying a tray filled with food. Terry had seen her around but had never spoken to her.

She took a look at Granger and frowned. She didn't seem to recognize him.

Then she looked down at herself. Her Personage was off, but she looked almost the same, except for a slight case of acne. She was dressed in a tattered housedress.

Granger croaked out, "Kirrie?" Then he turned and ran from the room. She watched him, puzzled.

Then Terry remembered where he'd seen Kirrie before. She'd been with Granger, apparently his assistant. Obviously, she'd never seen him without his Personage.

"What's happening?" Kirrie asked, looking around. Her gaze landed on Millard and she let out a little squeak. "I was hoping to serve you breakfast in bed, milord," she said.

Millard looked momentarily startled, then said smoothly, "I wanted an early start on the day, milady. But I thank you for the thought. Do you mind if Terry and I have that?" He stepped forward with his hands out, and she put the tray in them, looking disappointed. She braved a smile.

Her smiled brightened as her Personage flickered back on. Her skin was now flawless, her hair perfection. She leaned forward and whispered into Millard's ear, and Terry was probably the only one to overhear her say, "I had a lovely night."

Well, that explains why Granger hates Millard, he thought. It wasn't envy; it was pure jealousy.

Everyone had turned on their Personages, and suddenly the room was brighter and cleaner. A conversational hum filled the air, and it was as if everyone had already forgotten the strange little incident.

But Millard hadn't.

He walked over to a lone table and set down the tray. "Let's eat fast," he said. "I think Mr. Lundy and I need to confer."

Chapter 14

My daughter shows signs of being a leader; that is, if being bossy is any indication. She orders about the staff, her father, and most of all, me. She is so cute that most do as she says. I'm the only one who can deny her. I fear that when I'm gone, she'll immediately take over Spell Realm, though she is not yet a teenager. Currently, she's in a stereotypically "girly" stage, and everything needs to be pink and frilly. I shudder at the thought.

But she's also good-hearted, and more often than not, her orders are to the benefit of one of her playmates or one of the employees. She'll keep Halor engaged in the running of the business, or so I hope. Halor wants to send her off-world for her education, but I'm afraid if that happens, the fearless little girl we know will come back changed.

— Martinique Mansing

Shara had grown up in the second-tallest tower of Castle La Magie, topped only by her father's rooms atop the main spire. A narrow corridor offset her tower, which she called the Princess Tower, with its soft pastel colors and frilly embellishments. She shared a landing with her father, though by luck or design, she rarely encountered him.

By luck or design by her father or by her, she wasn't sure. She sensed when he was near, but it was rare nowadays that she felt like talking to him. He'd be pleasant enough at first, but eventually he'd get around to lecturing her about how she was wasting her life, she'd have to defend herself, his voice would rise, her voice would rise higher, and it would almost always end with both of them stonily silent.

Truth was, Shara was rarely in her tower. The oversized round bed with its pink and rose blankets, the white carpet, and the beige walls that had delighted her as a young girl were now off-putting. She'd been such a stereotypical old-fashioned princess. It made her gag.

She'd assigned herself servant's quarters on sublevel four. No one had told her she couldn't do it. She had never been given an official position in Spell Realm, other than founder's daughter. But one day she'd shown up at the reception desk, dressed as an off-world seasonal worker, having shorn her hair and eschewed makeup, and no one had recognized her. To her secret delight, she'd been teased and hassled just like all the other newbies, and she'd managed to hold her temper long enough to be accepted.

And then when, after a few months, she'd showed up late for work, expecting to be scolded, instead Granger Hovey had avoided her eyes. She walked up to his tall, gangly form and stood there until he had to look down at her, and the moment he did, she knew the gig was up.

"Don't tell anyone," she pleaded.

"I…uh…I won't," he said. "But…"

"But you already have," she answered for him, her heart falling.

She almost retreated to the Princess Tower then, but instead decided to still act as if she was still Shara from off-world, and if anyone dared talk to her differently, she glared at them until they stopped.

But it was never the same. When she saw something going wrong and made a suggestion, to her surprise, it was immediately carried out. Since she saw *a lot* wrong with the way things were being done, she couldn't resist. By the time her father found out, she was firmly in charge.

"I hire people to do that," he had said. "Experts in their field."

"Yeah, well, they suck at it," she'd said. "Tell me things haven't improved."

Since it was undeniable that things were running more smoothly, that customer complaints were down and revenues up, Shara's father left her in charge of the hotel. Not officially, but no one questioned it.

It was clear that no one had made any changes to Castle La Magie in a long time. There had been a brief flurry of improvements when her father married Millard's mother, but when she left, things started to fall apart again.

Shara took it upon herself to examine every part of the hotel and make changes. Her father intervened only once—when she tried to rent out her own rooms as the "Princess Suite."

"Someday you'll want it back," he said, and he would brook no argument.

At the entrance of Castle La Magie, there was a map on a plaque. Shara had walked by it a thousand times, ten thousand times, barely glancing at it. One day, she stopped and stared at it. Did it serve any real purpose? Did it add anything to the décor? She watched the foot traffic for a few days and was satisfied that enough guests stopped and examined it to make it useful. Then she really looked at it herself, pretending she was a guest and didn't know anything about Castle La Magie's layout.

It occurred to her that either the map was poorly drawn, which was doubtful since it appeared to come from an architect's schematic, or there was unaccounted-for space in the Princess Tower. Not much space, but enough to make her curious.

Shara began exploring, starting on the first floor. At the end of every corridor was a blank wall—until she reached the tenth floor, about halfway up the castle. There she found a small door. It was barely noticeable because a large potted tree hid it. Even then, she might not have noticed it if the tapestry that normally covered it hadn't fallen down.

She could barely squeeze past the tree. The door was locked, of course. It took her several more days before she managed to pick the lock and open it, because she had to break off every time anyone entered the hallway. This door had been hidden on purpose, and she doubted her father wanted her to find it.

Eventually, she got the door open and poked her head into the space beyond it. A dry, musty odor wafted from inside, the smell of time and neglect. Cobwebs snagged her hair, and she started coughing, so loudly that a guest came out of his room and stared at her curiously. She smiled at the man, closed the door, and walked away.

Next time, Shara brought a flashlight and a hat, and wore her oldest clothing.

As she approached the hidden door, she tried to keep her hopes down. It might be an abandoned maintenance closet, after all. There were lots of unexplainable nooks and crannies in Castle La Magie (though she was starting to wonder if there were other hidden rooms and corridors).

She looked over her shoulder to make sure she was alone, squeezed past the tree, and opened the door, stepping inside before she could change her mind. She flicked on the flashlight.

Stairs.

Not brooms or mops, but a narrow flight of stairs leading up. Holding one arm out in front of her to catch the cobwebs, she started climbing.

The steps spiraled upward tightly and seemed to be sized for her feet. They also seemed to go on forever, and after she had climbed what she estimated to be several floors high, she began to guess where they would lead.

Finally, at the top, there was a trapdoor. Shara put her palm against it, expecting it to be locked, or at least covered by something heavy.

The door easily flopped open, and she saw that she'd been wrong. It did not lead to the Princess Suite. It was another room, with dimensions so similar to her own quarters that she suspected that it was immediately below them. Not once in all her years growing up had she suspected such a thing existed.

The room was clear of dust and cobwebs, and everything was neat and tidy; a long desk against the far wall, bookshelves along two other walls, and a sofa and chair in the middle of the room. The fourth wall was full of maps and diagrams. She went to this wall first, already guessing what she'd find.

They were the plans for Spell Realm, and she sensed they'd existed before the park was built. Even a cursory glance showed her that they were different from the reality. She wandered to the bookshelves, examined the books, and realized that they were ancient, printed when books were how people still gained knowledge, maybe even from Old Earth.

Finally, she went to the long desk, which was filled with notebooks, most of them containing the same diagrams as those on the wall but in finer detail.

One large volume sat open in the middle of the desk, with the chair pushed up against the table at that spot. She leaned over it and started to read.

Chapter 15

Without my husband's invention of Flexstone, Spell Realm wouldn't have been possible. There is no doubting his genius, and even with the knowledge that such a technological advance is possible, his competitors have far to go to catch up.

It may seem silly to use such advanced technology in the service of pleasure and fantasy, but both of us have had quite enough of the real world.

Therefore, we have decided to keep our secrets on our own world, and to give pleasure to others, knowing full well that in time, Flexstone or something very like it will be used for less altruistic purposes.

— Martinique Mansing

As Millard and Terry approached the arena, they heard the crowd's screams. Terry resisted the impulse to run toward the sound. The Darke Dragon circled above. Humbert was fully repaired, a black shadow in the sky with fiery greens and reds flickering through his wings. Bursts of flame lit the already bright day, almost too brilliant to look at.

As they approached, though, Terry began to realize that something wasn't quite right. It wasn't until he reached the entrance to the arena that he realized that the dragon was not swooping down on the audience, close enough that its digital fire could have singed their hair had the flames been real. No, the dragon was circling just outside the seating area, swirling so fast and so menacingly that no one realized they weren't getting the full effect.

With one last roar, the dragon flew up into the clouds,

where a burst of light radiated across the sky and a thunderclap drowned out the cheers of the crowd.

Terry and Millard stood to one side as the excited tourists exited the arena. Only when the last of them was out of sight did the dragon reappear, floating quietly out of the sky, his wings no longer lit up, no fire emanating from his snout.

Humbert landed more roughly than Terry had ever seen him land before, his massive claws digging divots into the grass. Then the Darke Dragon lay down, lowered his head, and was still. Carl Lundy was furiously operating his workpad, frowning and muttering to himself.

"What's wrong?" Terry asked.

Carl jumped and swore. "Damn, don't sneak up on me like that."

Now Terry was certain something was terribly wrong. Carl was an easygoing boss, taking most things in stride. "Is there something wrong with Humbert?" he repeated.

"Obviously, but hell if I know what," Carl muttered, his attention once again on his workpad.

"May I see?" Millard asked.

Carl looked over at him, then silently handed the pad over as if admitting defeat.

"When did this start happening?" Millard asked.

"Off and on for the last week. Then, yesterday, Humbert almost crashed. I barely had enough warning to land him. A few hours later, the entire grid shut down. So, you tell me."

"Is that why you were flying him outside his normal pattern?" Terry asked.

Carl nodded. "I didn't want him crashing down on our guests. Bad for business. I lost three harpies this morning. Just came plunging out of the sky, so mangled they can't be repaired. I've grounded all the flying flex-creatures."

"The Personages shut down for a time this morning," Terry offered. "Did you notice that?"

"No," Carl answered. He wore the costume of a squire, but he otherwise made few sartorial concessions to Spell Realm. He didn't have a Personage, or if he did, he never wore it. No one dared give him demerits.

Terry looked over Millard's shoulder as his friend swiped through the charts too fast for him to follow. Millard's hand froze, and then he swiped back three charts and stared. "Have you noticed the Fanchon Particle spikes over the last month?"

"That's why I sent for you," Carl said. "You seem to be a wizard at extrapolating from limited data. What do you think it means? I'm wondering if Flexstone is particularly vulnerable to it."

Millard shook his head. "No more than any other nanoelectrical device, I would think."

"Is it coming from Solorum?" Terry asked. He'd once seen the local star outside the environmental envelope, and it had been a tiny, dim thing, so unlike the magnified sun above Spell Realm.

Carl shook his head. "Nor is it coming from any of the local stars, as far out as I've been able to check."

Millard's hand went to his mouth, his fingers ticking against his cheek, which is what he did when he was deep in thought.

But Terry thought there was an obvious question. "Did Placers Planet have an increase in Fanchon Particles before… you know…before *it* happened?" The catastrophe had occurred hundreds of years ago, but every schoolkid was taught about it. An entire mining settlement wiped out in an instant by a single burst. There were those who thought such massive events were why humanity had yet to find another spacefaring species—that no civilization had survived long enough to make it to the stars.

"They had a heavy atmosphere and a strong magnetic field," Carl answered. It was clear that he'd been wondering the same thing. "There would have been no reason to monitor Fanchon Particles. In fact, I don't think they knew what they were."

"I thought we had a shield for that," Terry said.

"There is no shield strong enough to withstand a Fanchon Particle burst," Millard said. "There would be no warning for the main event, either. The burst would arrive at the speed of light."

"'There is no warning,'" Terry intoned. "'Death's message is delivered by Death's own hand.'"

"What's that?" Carl asked.

"It's what Lamiere wrote about it," Terry said.

"Lamiere?" Carl echoed.

"Placers Planet's last poet laureate, before it was abandoned. He was on the Hamilton, the last ship to leave—you know, the one that disappeared."

Millard shivered. "Spooky. Fortunately, the phenomenon has been studied extensively since then. Well, I think that's our answer. We must evacuate Spell Realm."

Both Terry and Carl froze, though both had been thinking the same thing.

"Isn't that a little drastic?" Carl asked after a time.

"We'd better get ahold of my stepfather," Millard said. He looked momentarily confused, then shook his head. "I left my workpad with...at the workshop. You got his number, Mr. Lundy?"

"I do, but..." Carl said, his voice drifting off as if he realized he was really going to have to call. He handed his workpad over to Millard. "But only for emergencies."

"Yeah, well," Millard said. "Doesn't get much more of an emergency than this."

"You realize this could be the end of Spell Realm," Terry said, his heart heavy. This morning, he'd woken up thinking everything was normal, and now his world was crashing down.

"One way or the other," Millard agreed, seeming almost cheerful about it. He continued to leaf through the workpad, so fast that Terry couldn't even ascertain the subject of one page before his friend was on to the next. Suddenly he stopped, leaned closer to the pad, and stared at a graph. "It appears that we are not the first to wonder about this phenomenon," Millard said. "A Professor Edgar Walker investigated the Fanchon Particle record of Placers Planet twenty-five years after the event."

Carl came over and stood on one side of Millard while Terry stood on the other. Millard found the graph of the last few days of Fanchon Particle readings on Spell Realm and overlaid them on those from the last few days of Placers Planet's existence. They were a perfect match.

"All right," Carl sighed. "I'll call Mr. Mansing."

Carl put out his hand, and Millard passed back the workpad.

The old man activated the speaker and the phone connected. On the other end, the phone started ringing. Terry expected it to go to messaging, but it just kept ringing. Finally, Carl clicked off, shrugging.

"Come now, you must have a way of reaching him in emergencies," Millard said mildly.

"He told me to never use that number unless…"

Humbert shuddered behind them, his tail flicking and nearly sweeping them off their feet. A loud hum arose, and then Humbert opened his snout and a sound emerged that was supposed to be a roar, but instead sounded like death rattle.

Humbert had been quiescent before, but he had still seemed alive. Now, Terry sensed, he was nothing but Flexstone and wiring.

Carl quickly dialed again.

"This better be damned important," Mansing's imperious voice answered. "I'm talking to my daughter."

"Sir, we need to evacuate Spell Realm."

There was total silence. When Mansing finally spoke, he sounded calm and measured. "What did you say?"

"Sir, we think that…"

The workpad blinked off. All around them, the lights went out, and there was a sudden chill, not only from the outside but from the inside. It appeared that every machine in Spell Realm had stopped working at the same time.

Seconds later, Castle La Magie lit up as the backup generators kicked in, but only the castle. The rest of Spell Realm remained dark, even though, within the illusion of the park, it had been midday. Sirens blared, loud enough to make Terry jump.

"It appears we're too late," Millard said.

"It isn't safe here," Carl said. "Let's get back to the castle." The old man started off, not looking back. Terry began to follow, but Millard grabbed his hand. "I need to get back to the lab," he said.

"Now?"

"I want to talk to…that other guy. Maybe he knows what's going on. Besides, I don't trust him. He seems devious."

Terry couldn't help himself. He laughed.

"What?"

"He *is* you, Millard. You mean you don't trust yourself?"

"He isn't anything *like* me," Millard said.

Terry studied his friend, marveling that such a smart man could be so blind. "If you must go, hurry. The castle might be the only safe place here."

"Unless we do something about it," Millard said.

"Like what?"

Millard gave Terry a knowing look, then turned away. "There may be a way," Terry heard him murmur as he hurried off.

Chapter 16

The creatures of Spell Realm must appear to be dangerous, and for that to happen, they must be dangerous; at least, enough for both the hunter and the hunted to believe it so. (Which is the hunter and which is the hunted is up the guest, of course.)

A creature must be programmed in such a way that it believes it is striking the killing blow, and yet will always miss. The guest, as a result, will believe it also.

The occasional accident would not be untoward, as long as the ensuing publicity results in enough increased visits to cover the insurance premiums.

— Martinique Mansing

Mary Peterson blocked out Eddy's nattering worries. She wasn't about to cut short her visit, even though Eddy kept glancing back at Castle La Magie's spire, barely visible above the forest canopy. They'd heard an alarm a while back, but it had taken her two weeks to reach Spell Realm, two weeks she could ill afford to waste. Besides, she was fine. There had been a moment when she couldn't catch her breath and a cold breeze had blown over her, but then her Personage had let out a little whirr and the heat and the oxygen had kicked in.

The light was dimmer than before, and there had been a panicky minute or two when the castle behind them plunged into darkness, but then the lights had come back on. They could still follow the path. The drake's tracks were becoming deeper and clearer with every step.

The drake was close, she could tell.

Eddy was riding an old, fat mare, though he probably wasn't even aware he was being condescended to by being given this steed. They'd tried to foist an equally docile animal on Mary, but she'd quickly let them know that she knew how to ride very well, thank you very much. The guide had bowed obsequiously, but she could tell he was secretly impressed. He'd brought out a young stallion who had reared up at the sight of the saddle, and that had been just right. She'd quickly let the horse know who was boss.

"You must be careful, Sir Edward, Lady Mary," the guide had said, pointing in the direction of the forest. "It is said that a drake has recently spawned a new hatch of eggs. The young beasts are terribly dangerous."

Then he'd winked at them, which had rather ruined the effect.

Eddy couldn't seem to sit comfortably on his steed, and his armor clanked every time he moved. When Mary had first met him, his enthusiasm for all things medieval had been endearing and even contagious. This trip had been his idea, and she'd decided it would be a good way to take his measure, to see what he was like outside the office.

So far, she wasn't impressed.

Her costume choices had included a princess gown with an accompanying carriage, but she had chosen the ranger costume, a forest green tunic and leggings that she could easily maneuver in. Eddy had chosen a suit of armor and the biggest sword and shield he could find (and had been complaining ever since about how heavy they were). Mary had taken a short sword—or a large dagger, she wasn't sure which it was supposed to be.

There was a roar to their left, and Eddy's fat old horse reared. Eddy tumbled backward off the mare with a clatter.

Mary hopped off her own horse and ran to his side. She'd read the park contract all the way through and knew that falling off a horse wasn't covered. He groaned and sat up.

The drake stepped out of the trees. If much smaller than the Darke Dragon, it was bigger than Mary had expected, about the size of her horse. There were green scales along its back and yellow ridges across its broad chest. It had two stunted wings that she doubted were functional, a long, narrow tail, and two heads with long snouts bristling with teeth.

One for each of us, she thought. How thoughtful.

Sir Edward lumbered to his feet, drew his sword, and clomped toward the beast, which reared up on its hind legs and breathed fire down on his hastily erected shield.

Impressive, Mary thought. If only it were real, she'd be delighted with both her prey and her prospective beau.

She looked for somewhere to tie up her stallion, but he jerked the reins out of her hand and ran off. Apparently, the horses weren't in on the trick.

Damn. It was a long ride back, but the old, fat mare could probably hold them both. She drew her shortsword and hurried to Eddy's side. He was raining blows on the creature, which dodged them easily, darting forward while Eddy was off balance and snapping at him. Each time, she thought Eddy was done for, but he always managed to twist away.

One of the drake's heads turned toward her, spitting fire. Mary jumped to one side and felt the heat singe her hair. It was close enough, dangerous enough to feel real, and she felt a surge of energy. She leapt forward and thrust with her sword, and skewered the drake's head. Its eyes rolled up and the head dropped, tipping the beast to one side, leaving an opening for even Eddy's slow lunges. He drove the blade of his sword into the drake's chest to its hilt.

"Yes!" he cried, pumping his gauntleted fist.

Mary smiled. It was nice. He was nice. Maybe he really was the one.

She leaned over the drake's head she'd skewered and started cutting it off.

"Should we be doing that?" Eddy asked. "It'll cost extra."

Big deal. She was paying for the trip, after all. As she sliced, she caught sight of little wires withdrawing into the drake's body, the only sign that it was artificial. She lifted the head triumphantly, wondering if she should have it stuffed.

Eddy's smile disappeared. He was looking at something behind her. Mary whirled, sword in hand.

At first she couldn't see it; then the steady movement caught her eye. It was a snake, smaller than the drake but still huge, and there was something about it that sent a chill down her spine. It wasn't moving sinuously side to side like a snake but seemed to be floating along the ground. In the dim light, she caught sight of hundreds of tiny legs.

What kind of fantasy creature is this? I thought I knew them all.

She stepped forward, intending to stab the creature in the head as she had the drake, but then she caught a glimpse of its mouth. It was round and ringed by hundreds of thin, needlelike teeth.

"Mary, I don't think we should mess with it," Eddy said uneasily.

The creature surged toward her, and she let out a shout, tried to retreat, and tripped. The ring-toothed mouth was only inches away. Then an armored foot stomped down on the creature, stopping it. Eddy swung downward with his blade.

Mary was impressed. She'd have expected Eddy to run; instead, he'd stepped up. This trip wasn't a waste after all. She'd finally found a man she could respect.

The blade bounced off the creature's head.

Eddy cried out and lost his footing, stumbling to the side. The snake reared up, and its mouth opened wider. It kept rising higher and higher, and then dropped straight down, the ring of teeth covering Eddy's helmeted head. Mary heard a muffled, dismayed shout, and then the creature's mouth closed. Eddy's headless body flopped to the ground.

Mary was up and running before she was aware of deciding to move. Castle La Magie's lights beckoned in the distance. She looked over her shoulder but saw no movement along the ground. It was only as she began to turn her head back toward the path in front of her that she saw something flying toward her.

The snake had sprouted three sets of wings, looking like a huge dragonfly, its teeth now red with blood. She turned and ran faster, then felt something strike her in the back hard enough to throw her on the ground.

She couldn't move. Her face was in the dirt, and she could barely breathe. She could hear the creature tearing into her flesh, and her body rocked from side to side, but she couldn't feel anything.

This is real, she thought wonderingly.

The creature tossed her onto her back. Mary felt it crawling up her chest, and its mouth came into view. Her scream filled the air, and then the mouth came down and the night went silent.

Chapter 17

Even given the increased acreage I insisted upon, it is of course impossible to have a complete ecosystem, as much as I might like one. It would be preferable to have the wild animals imported to this world be self-sufficient, to wander through the forests and grasslands as if completely free.

We won't be able to grow enough to feed all the animals, so we will be forced to bring fodder in from off-world.

However, I don't want Spell Realm to feel like a zoo. It must appear natural, and for that to happen, there must be wildlife that the fantasy creatures we will create will feed upon. A dragon must take an occasional deer or antelope, after all.

Of course, the Flexstone creatures won't actually be eating anything, so we will need to be careful about population control, perhaps allow hunting on the part of our guests—as long as they use proper weapons, such as bows and arrows, swords, or spears.

If it was up to me, I'd have lions and tigers and bears, too. But I've been told that having an occasional guest eaten is bad for business.

— Martinique Mansing

When Mill woke up, the woman was gone. He lay back in the firm bed and soft sheets, trying to remember her name. Kirrie, that was it. She'd given herself freely to him, asking nothing in return—at least, nothing immediately. It was clear that she hoped that he would like her, perhaps enough to be his girlfriend or even wife. Apparently, unlike a lowly apprentice wizard, his double was someone important in this world, the son of the prince, or what passed for a prince in what they called "Spell Realm."

An ironic name, at least to Mill, since there was little magic here. Nothing like his own home, Munsury.

Or…maybe there was. Because the more he'd talked to Millard the previous day, the more he'd felt that they were doing exactly the same thing, using different words, perhaps, but the same formulas. Millard called it "mathematics," but Mill recognized proportions that were almost exactly the same as in the magic spells of his own world. They used numbers here in the familiar way, for counting things. But then they twisted the numbers and combined them with letters and symbols until it became something much larger.

And yet, Mill recognized in the patterns the making of magic. The difference seemed to be that here, simply knowing the words was not enough. Here, they needed mechanical and chemical processes to reach the same ends.

It seemed primitive and crude, and yet…

He stretched out again and ran his hands along the surface of the bed. These sheets had a far tighter weave than any on his world. He'd quizzed Kirrie after coupling with her, and though she'd been puzzled by his questions, she'd answered them. (Apparently, Millard was thought odd in this land, so odd questions weren't out of place.)

Whereas in Munsury, everyday items were handmade one by one, in this world, they produced the same item the same way over and over again. Because of the expertise they had developed, the same processes were used to do such things as build roads and bridges, to travel, to raise crops, and to fight disease. Because such mass production only worked if everyone was involved, all shared in the bounty.

Oh, there was rich and there was poor in this land. There was nobility and servitude (thought they didn't call it that). But even the poorest had luxuries that even princes of Munsury lacked.

Magic has made us lazy, Mill thought. Wizards were called upon to do big things: raise castles, move rivers, and bring down mountains. If something smaller and more localized needed to be done, there were hedge wizards who knew just enough magic to do it. It had never occurred to the people of his land to produce enough of a single item to make it available to all.

There was much to learn here. At first, Mill had wanted to immediately return to his own world, but the longer he stayed, the more he realized that there were things here that would be useful to know.

His "overalls" were draped over a chair. He rose from the bed and crossed the room. As he lifted the one-piece clothing, he noticed a note on the desk.

"Have gone to get breakfast. Be right back."

Amazing. He'd already known that the language of Spell Realm was the same as Munsury's, but he'd never expected even the writing to be the same. If he could track down the grimoires of this Spell Realm so that he might learn its secrets, he wouldn't need to ask ignorant servants odd questions.

"P.S.," said the note. "You left your sweater here last time."

Under the overalls, there was another item of clothing. It appeared to be made of finer material. Since it seemed that the overalls, which he'd wore the previous day, were looked down upon, he donned the sweater, which was soft and warm.

Mill made for the door. He had no desire to continue talking to Kirrie, whom he'd quickly discovered was lacking in the kind of knowledge he desired.

The hallway outside her room was long, lined with numbered doors. Again, such duplication seemed efficient and strangely impersonal. He had figured out that this world had a much larger population than where he came from. Indeed, this Spell Realm was apparently nothing more than a park, created for the amusement of their nobility, but already, he'd seen more people in one place than he'd ever seen in his life.

He approached what Kirrie had called the elevator. She'd "reminded" him that she lived "fifteen floors down," which, from the gut-sinking motion of the little room, he guessed meant that they had gone downward fifteen floors of the castle. It was apparently everyday magic to her but would have been a wonder in Munsury.

The elevators door conveniently opened as he neared it and a young couple emerged, laughing. They fell silent at the sight of him and gave him a strange look. Mill looked down at himself.

Only the sweater was different from the day before, so apparently it wasn't appropriate, for whatever reason. But they didn't say anything, simply nodded respectfully, so he suspected that Millard could wear anything at all and people would overlook it.

He entered the elevator and stared at the numbers. A light illuminated the number fifteen, and he deduced that he wanted to go to number one and pressed it.

"Hold the door!" someone shouted.

Mill had no idea how to do that and just stood there stupidly as a young man ran toward him. The doors started to close, but the newcomer put out his arms, and when the door struck his hands, it retreated. (Yet more magic!)

The young man was about Mill's own age, and he acted as if they were friends. Mill forced a smile. "Sorry," he said.

"No problem," the stranger answered, though he was obviously a little miffed. He looked Mill up and down with a strange expression. "Are you chilly, Millard?"

"What's that?"

"The sweater."

"Oh, I just didn't want to carry it," Mill answered. "I left it in Kirrie's room."

A look of surprise came over the young man's face. "Kirrie? I thought…" Then he seemed to think better of it and shut up.

"And you are?" Millard asked.

"Pardon?"

"Your name, sir."

The man flushed. "I'm Cleve. We were classmates together, Millard. Don't you remember?"

"I've been working very hard," Mill said. "I'm tired and I haven't slept. Please forgive me."

"We worked together just a week ago on Horny," Cleve continued, obviously aggrieved.

"Horny?"

"Oh, I know we aren't supposed to use that name," Cleve said. "The unicorn…sir." Cleve added the title was as if he thought he was in some kind of trouble.

"Of course," Mill said, as if it was of no importance. "Tell me, Cleve. Where can I find grimoires and–"

"Grimoires?" Cleve blurted, so flustered he was almost speechless.

"Books about how things work," Mill explained. The little tablet that Millard kept tapping contained all the information that existed, apparently. But Mill had no idea how to operate one, nor did he have one at hand. How to use one of these devices was the first thing he was going to learn.

Now Cleve *was* speechless. He stared at Mill, mouth open.

"I recently took a blow to the head," Mill said, thinking fast. "During the blackout."

"Ohhhhh!" Cleve said, as if that cleared up everything. Now he looked concerned. "Maybe you should go to the infirmary, Millard. You know, Sali is in charge of that now. You… uh…remember her, don't you?"

"I'm fine," Mill said, trying to keep the annoyance out of his voice. "Please answer my question."

"Sure, sure," Cleve said, swallowing. "I'll lead you to the library. Though I'd have thought that was the last thing you'd forget. I swear you spent more time there than you did at school. None of us could believe you got away with it. But then, you were always…" He trailed off as if he was afraid of finishing the thought.

"Yes?" Mill asked.

"You were always smarter than us," Cleve admitted.

Undoubtedly, Mill thought. If Millard is as superior to the ordinary folk as I am in my own world, there is hardly any common ground between us and them. It made him feel better to realize it. He suspected that no matter how strange he acted, it would be covered up by these underlings' awe.

Cleve reached past Mill and punched a symbol he wasn't familiar with—it had three upright IIIs. The young wizard quickly figured out that the symbols above the numbers he recognized were also numbers, but in a different language. He guessed that III meant they were going up to the third level of the castle.

Soon, they were standing in front of two doors, which swung open at their approach. Cleve stopped short. "Joan Hambil is still in charge, you know," he said. "Just saying."

Mill nodded, not sure how to answer.

"Well, I'll see you around, Millard," Cleve said.

"Thank you for your help." Mill knew it sounded overly formal, but he had no idea how to talk to Cleve. At home, he had no equals. He had his superiors, such Lumbli and the nobles that they both served, but other than that, there was no one he felt familiar enough with to exchange casual pleasantries with.

"All right," Cleve said. "Take care of yourself."

Mill sighed and entered the library. An old woman stood up from behind a desk, her shock plain on her face. "Millard?" she asked, as if she couldn't believe it.

"Hello," Mill said. Apparently, this woman knew him. The less he said, the better. "I would like to look at books about mathematics, chemistry, and engineering."

Joan Hambil laughed. "You've already memorized everything in here, Millard."

"I...of course. I believe I've found some errors. I'd like to check."

"Oh," she said. She thought about this for a moment and then seemed to decide it wasn't unusual that a young man would doubt the accuracy of the written word. "Which ones would you like to start with?"

"If you don't mind, the same order in which I read them the first time."

She demurred no longer and came back with a stack of books. He opened the top one and started reading.

This stack alone was more books than he'd ever seen in one place.

Machines did this. Knowledge available to anyone, even the lowest commoner.

He tried a couple of learning spells, and to his surprise, they worked.

The worlds are bleeding into each other.

It was obvious from the incredulous looks the librarian kept giving him that turning a page every couple of seconds or so wasn't normal. She had a determined smile on her face, which in his experience meant she didn't like him. No, not him; Millard.

Well, I can understand. Millard does seem like a rude fellow.

The morning and afternoon sped by. It wasn't until the lights went out that Mill wondered what time it was. From the librarian's distressed cry, he deduced that such darkness was not normal. He reached inside himself for a lighting spell, and for a second, a light formed in the palm of his hand. It blinked out at the same moment the overheads lights came on.

Mill thought he now understood the machine that his doppelgänger had built. There was a flaw, however. It was obvious when one understood the…what was it called? Science.

He closed the book and, without saying a word to the old lady, left the library. He needed to see Millard immediately.

It was odd that no one had come looking for him. In his own world, no one was allowed to just go anywhere they wanted.

This world gets stranger by the moment.

If his double was anything like Mill, he'd be in the work shed, working on his device.

Chapter 18

Spell Realm has only one true competitor.

The Morgana Corporation, founded by an Arthurian fiction fan club, is actually older than we are. But because they do not have the formula to use Flexstone for anything other than building material, they are forced to use illusions, holograms, and virtual reality much more than we do.

For the real experience, for the feeling that everything is solid, you must come to Spell Realm. There are no wavering, transparent images here, no will-o'-the-wisps or ghost lights. When you touch a creature here, it has density and texture.

Over time, no matter how spectacular the illusions that holographic technology can create, nothing beats the "real" thing.

We are a constant target of corporate espionage—and most of it originates from Morgana. I feel almost sorry for them.

— Martinique Mansing

"**W**here is she, Caleb?" Selene asked for the fourth time that day.

Caleb had been certain he could track down Shara in a short time. He knew her schedule and her favorite spots. But she was nowhere to be found.

"She must not be in Castle La Magie," he said, finally.

"Where else would she be?"

Caleb knew that his future was becoming more precarious by the second. He wouldn't put it past the sisters to dump him and go off on their own. Not only would that look bad to his bosses at Morgana Corp., but he'd hoped to be able to protect

Shara by being present during every moment of her captivity—whether she liked it or not.

"She occasionally rides in the Mossy Forest," he said, thinking aloud. "Or perhaps she's at the spaceport." Neither of those locations seemed likely to him, but he had to offer something.

He'd once followed her to the back of the castle, where she had disappeared. After searching, he had found a hidden door behind a tapestry. He'd been stymied by the locked door, accessible only to employees. Anyone else the Morgana Corp. might have sent would've picked the lock, but to Caleb, a locked door was as good as a law.

He had hurried around the side of the castle, finding storage units and wild meadows behind it, but hadn't glimpsed Shara. Wherever she'd gone, he'd lost her.

The three sisters were staring at him impatiently. He'd already learned that the differences between them were superficial, more a pose than a reality. Despite Marie's smiles, there was little goodwill in her. Despite Selene's scowls, she wasn't any more negative than the other two. Despite Trina's dark looks, she moved and acted just like her sisters.

"There are four of us," he said. "We can split the park into quadrants, see what we can find. She has to be somewhere."

The three sisters hesitated, obviously uncomfortable about splitting up. *Something to remember.*

"Very well," Trina said. "Show us where to search."

He sent her toward the Mossy Forest, Marie to the spaceport, and Selene to the tournament grounds. He saved the space behind Castle La Magie for himself, since he figured that's where Shara was most likely to be. He was still uncertain about warning her, but perhaps, if he got her alone...

He headed around the side of Castle La Magie. The tournament grounds were close, but there was a narrow corridor between them and the castle. He saw someone approaching on a scooter and started to concoct an explanation for his presence, but the young squire aboard the scooter simply raised his hand in salute and shot on by.

The light beyond the tunnel got brighter, and finally he

stepped onto grass, roughly cropped by the livestock that dotted the grounds. He walked carefully, avoiding the cow pies and horse droppings, and found a path that led to the outbuildings.

As he stepped onto the path, someone approached him from behind.

Caleb turned around and froze. He recognized the young man. It was the child genius, Millard. The boy barely looked at him, almost passing by before pausing to ask, "You lost, pal?"

"I'm sorry," Caleb said. "Is this area restricted?"

Millard considered this. "I don't know, actually. But you have no reason to be here."

"I just had to get away from the fantasy, at least for a short while. It's a little overwhelming, you know what I mean?"

Millard broke into a smile. "I understand. We have a saying around here: 'Reality is for those who can't handle fantasy.'"

"Ha!" Caleb said, nodding. "Well, that's me, I guess."

"It may not be safe out here," Millard warned. "Haven't you heard the sirens?"

"I'll take my chances."

Millard examined him for a few more moments, then apparently decided he was harmless. He turned around and walked on, waving as he left. "Well, don't spook the horses!" he called over his shoulder.

Caleb waited until the young man disappeared into a small shed before following him, now certain he was on the right track. While they weren't especially close, Shara did visit her stepbrother occasionally—or more likely, that young man who was a friend of Millard's, Terry something.

He heard voices from inside the shed. Well, one voice, seeming to have a conversation with itself. *You know what they say about geniuses*, he thought wryly.

The shelter was a crude structure; the planks were not flush with each other. He put his eye to a crack.

At first, he thought it was an optical illusion, some kind of pinhole effect. But as he noticed that the two figures were dressed differently and moved separately, he realized that there were two people inside.

Both of them were Millard Mansing.

Caleb stepped back, rubbing his eyes and shaking his head. Then moved up to the crack again.

There was no doubt about it. There were two Millard Mansings, arguing strenuously with each other. He could hear their words but couldn't make sense of them. It sounded like mathematics mixed with magic.

Again, he stepped back, trying to figure out what to do.

Nothing, he decided. As surreal as this was, it didn't matter. He was looking for Sharina Mansing, not her stepbrother—or stepbrothers. The Mayerling sisters would be waiting impatiently for him back at the castle. Maybe they'd had better luck.

As he turned to go, he saw a flash of deep green out of the corner of his eye. Behind the work shed was a green sky, and hanging in the midst of the unnaturally colored expanse were two moons, both of them larger than the facsimile moon that usually appeared above Spell Realm.

He blinked and rubbed his eyes again, and this time it worked. The green skies turned back to blue and the two moons disappeared.

Spell Realm had been a little buggy since he'd gotten there, with strange power outages and noises, but Caleb had figured that any place this complex would have its glitches. He hurried up the path, certain now that there was something seriously wrong with the place and that it was time to leave, with or without Shara Mansing in tow.

Calip led the Sister Executioners into the forest. In the distance, Castle La Magie stabbed the green horizon, the two moons on either side of its towers. For a moment, there was a flash of blue. He blinked and it was gone.

Magic. There were said to be powerful wizards in residence at Castle La Magie.

Just as long as I don't run into them. I hate wizards.

Lady Sharina was nowhere to be found, and the sisters were impatient. The Chance Knight could only think of one place she could've gone. He'd followed her into the forest twice before, and each time, she had stopped at a small pond covered by lily pads. There she had eaten a picnic lunch, serenaded by a boisterous chorus of frogs. The sojourns had served no purpose that he could see, but he had to admit, once you got used to it, the frog symphony was restful.

He motioned to the sisters to be quiet and kept walking. A short time later, he turned around, confused, certain that for some reason, they hadn't followed him. But they were at his heels, silent and nearly invisible. They had split up and blended in with the terrain, making no noise whatsoever; the dark sister upon the muddy path, the light sister among the yellow flowers that lined the trail, and the drab sister on the other side, the same color as the tree stumps.

Calip shivered involuntarily but continued on. He considered stumbling or coughing loudly to warn Lady Sharina of their approach but could think of no way to do so without losing all credibility with the sisters. He still needed them to trust him, at least until he could figure a way out of his dilemma.

The trail led to a tall stand of pussy willows, which he knew would hide their approach. The path then continued in a circle around the pond. On the other side was a small meadow with a large oak tree whose branches hung over the water. Lady Sharina would have spread her blanket upon the moist ground and be leaning back against the trunk while she ate.

The cacophony of the frogs stopped. Calip held up his hand, but it was unnecessary; the sisters had already frozen in place. He had to focus to make out their shapes.

Thank the blessed moons the Sister Executioners aren't after me, he thought.

The frogs started up again in full croak, as if there had never been an interruption. Calip and the sisters crept around the stand of pussy willows, and he crouched down, glancing toward the oak.

Lady Sharina was staring at the white blooms of the water lilies, chewing a sandwich thoughtfully. She was dressed all in white, with a blue sash around her waist. It was peasant clothing but looked like a palace gown on her.

Calip sensed rather than heard the sisters gather behind him.

"Is she alone?" Marifor whispered.

She is always alone, Calip almost answered, then wondered at the thought. It wasn't true in the literal sense, for Sharina had many friends, and yet she seemed to always be set apart, the lonely center of every crowd. "No one else comes here," he said.

"Can we approach from behind her?" Trinafor asked.

Calip shook his head. "The reeds surrounding the pond are impossible to get through."

"Then she has no escape," Selefor said. "Let's be about our business."

Before Calip could reply, the Sister Executioners were running. Marifor and Trinafor ran clockwise around the pond, while Selefor ran the other way. Reluctantly, Calip stood and followed.

Lady Sharina finally noticed them and stood hesitantly.

Run! Run away! Calip wanted to shout, and perhaps, if it could have done any good, he would have. But it was no use. Sharina was trapped.

The frogs fell quiet again. The air around them shimmered; the green sky took on an iridescent glow. The oak tree appeared to grow, to loom over them. Above, the moons quickened their stately pace, and the white of the water lilies became dazzling.

The three sisters didn't seem to notice, but kept charging. Calip watch them glide down the path, and it appeared to him that their feet didn't touch the ground, that they were flying. They seemed taller, their blades, which had been hidden in their tunics, now as long as swords. Each sister's colors deepened, so that Trinafor was a black shadow, Marifor a piercing yellow, and Selefor as brown as rain-swept earth.

The thick reeds behind the oak parted, and Calip saw that he had been wrong; there was a path there, wide and clear, a shining pavement of black stone. Down it galloped a blinding-white steed with black eyes and a long, thin horn on its forehead.

The unicorn reached Lady Sharina first, and she turned and lifted her hand. The unicorn reared and whinnied, louder than thunder, freezing Calip where he stood. The sisters kept coming, converging on Sharina at the same time.

The unicorn lowered his head, and his horn bled darkness, the point so sharp and black that no light could illuminate it.

Lady Sharina stood at the unicorn's shoulder.

The Sister Executioners all stopped at the same instant, just beyond reach of the horn.

"Surrender," Marifor cried. "We will not hurt you."

Lady Sharina didn't seem the slightest bit frightened. The unicorn and her dress were the same color—it was as if they had merged and were one creature. She looked across the pond into Calip's eyes, and he was certain he saw disappointment in hers.

Marifor stood just inches from the tip of the horn. Trinafor began to move to the left, while Selefor circled to the right. The unicorn shook his head, and his black mane rippled over his white coat like reeds in a current.

Sharina swept up onto the unicorn's back, and now they truly were one creature, shining as if from within. Before the sisters could reach them, the unicorn turned and galloped down the magical path, disappearing from view.

With a howl, dark and light, deep and high, the sisters tried to follow, but the path closed and the reeds blocked their way, and no amount of slashing with their knives could open it up again.

Calip sat down in the middle of the muddy path and bowed his head, but whether his legs had weakened from relief or from fear, he wasn't quite sure.

Chapter 19

My daughter will grow up in Castle La Magie. Halor and I will need to be careful that she understands that Spell Realm is not the real world, but a fantasy. It will be difficult, because for our concept to work, it must be completely immersive. How can a young girl who has known no other world than this be given an understanding of reality?

Halor wants to send Shara to an off-world school when she is old enough, though it will break my heart to be parted from her. Only when she has lived among others in a mundane world for a time will she return to enjoy Castle La Magie. I already ache from the thought of her being gone, and I already anticipate the look of joy she will have when she returns. For it is only when one has dealt with the drudgery of real life that one can truly appreciate the illusion.

— Martinique Mansing

Shara closed her mother's diary slowly, thoughtfully.

She'd never known her mother, who had died before Shara's memories were formed, but it was obvious her father had followed Martinique's instructions, sending Shara to Old Earth for school when she was only seven years old. It hadn't been as wrenching as her mother feared. Instead, it was the mundane world that was magical to her.

At least at first.

She'd found making friends easy. (They had all envied her living in Spell Realm.) Her studies had been even easier. Only in the dark of night did she remember Spell Realm, but the fantasy world seemed like something out of a storybook, something that had happened to someone else. When she returned for holidays, she scorned what she considered the silly pretense, spending most of her time inside Castle La Magie reading histories of real events, ignoring the Personages, mentally stripping away the masks and costumes for a glimpse of the real people behind them.

That Shara had no mother hadn't been unusual among her classmates. Half of them came from families with divorced parents, and really, what did it matter if they were just going to be sent away anyway? So she'd never felt especially deprived.

Then, one day, she'd come across a history of Spell Realm and learned that her mother had been at least as important to the establishment of the park as her father. After that, she'd scoured the library for references to Martinique Mansing, finding a volume of letters she'd written to her then fiancé. Flexstone had just been invented, and she was encouraging him to keep it secret and away from the giant corporations that owned most worlds.

Shara had never gotten a real sense of her mother until now. It was as if Martinique was speaking directly to her. Her presence was palpable in this hidden room. Though Shara wanted to keep reading, the words were fading in and out of focus from eye strain. She was only halfway through the diary. She glanced at the time and realized she'd read through the night and into the next day.

Standing and stretching, she looked up. Her eyes caught the outline of a trapdoor. Estimating its position in the room where she had spent her childhood, she guessed it must be directly beneath her round bed. She pulled a chair over to it and climbed up. She pushed upward, and the door popped open, raining dust. It slammed against the bottom of her childhood bed, leaving what appeared to be just enough space to crawl through. Shara sneezed, then shoved the diary into the gap. She poked her head through, lifted herself up, and squirmed through the trapdoor.

Her hair got caught on the tired springs of her old bed, and she carefully untangled herself. The light was dim. Unlike the clean room below, there were dust bunnies the size of her fist on the carpet. She didn't allow servants in her room. She sneezed again and then shimmied out from under the bed.

Daylight filtered through the curtains of the lone window. She had pushed an old sock out from under the bed, a pink, lacy thing she remembered from her teens. She stared down at the sock, feeling displaced. The familiar confines of her childhood were off-kilter, as if everything was in the wrong place.

Shara had heard that other kids feared monsters under their beds, but sometimes, just before she drifted off to sleep, she sensed that her mother was nearby, watching over her. She'd never questioned it. Magic surrounded her every day.

The first time she came home from school, that same feeling of nearness to her mother had crept over her. She'd leapt out of bed, dragging the blankets with her, and slept on the couch in the library next to her bedroom. She never told her father. Every morning, she returned the blankets to her room, mussing up the bed to fool the servants.

Her father had installed an elevator outside her room. Supposedly, he'd done it for her, but Shara rarely used it, preferring to climb the stairs like the workers were forced to do. Now she tried to remember the code, experimenting a little. Her birthday did the trick and the elevator quickly ascended, landing her directly in her father's den, bypassing the guard outside.

Her father was behind his broad desk, as usual. She glanced around, once again feeling that things were out of place, and realized that the room was cluttered. She'd never seen that before. Her father was fastidious, and what few messes he made, the servants quickly cleaned up. She had a feeling that no servant had been in this room for a long time.

Even more startling, her father was unshaven and blurry eyed. He stared at her, and she had the sense that it took him a few seconds to realize who she was. When was the last time she'd been here?

Months, she thought. *He's been meeting me in the formal dining room.*

Shara didn't let her disquiet stop her. She marched up to the desk and let the diary drop in front of Halor with a thud.

He looked up at her with a sigh. "I wondered how long it would be before you found it."

"You knew about it?"

But of course he'd known. The secret room had been spotless, everything in its place. And it hadn't been servants who cleaned it, she guessed. He was keeping it the way Martinique had left it, as a shrine.

"How far have you read?" he asked, picking up the book. The piece of torn paper she'd used as a bookmark fluttered to the floor. He opened the diary and read the entry.

"Ah, she was still inspired then," he said. He rubbed his eyes and smiled sadly at Shara. "I'm glad I have a chance to explain what happened."

"Explain?" Her voice rose. "You had this diary all along and you didn't show me?"

"I figured that when you were ready, it would happen," he said. "You have grown into a sensible young woman, so it appears I was correct."

"What right did you have to keep this from me?" The tone of her voice was unfamiliar, even to herself. She'd never been so angry.

The phone on the desk rang, but Halor ignored it. He started to stand, but then sat back as if he was too tired to make the effort. He said, "As you keep reading, perhaps you'll understand. But you should know, Shara, by the time your mother disappeared, we were barely speaking. If not for the diary, I'd have never known what was going on in her head."

"Disappeared?" Shara shouted. She'd been told her mother had died, that they'd found her outside the park, deep within a bergschrund. A tragic accident. "Known what, Father? What aren't you telling me?"

"Martinique disappeared," Halor said. He slumped in his chair and put his head in hands. "We never found her."

"But…then how do you know she's dead?"

"She has to be," he said in a low voice, without emotion. "I've spent a fortune looking for her. There wasn't a trace. You have to understand, Shara. I have wealth and resources you can't imagine. If she was alive, I'd have found her."

This time a different phone rang, and that caught her father's attention. He dug into his pocket and looked at the phone. To her disbelief, he answered it.

"This better be damned important. I'm talking to my daughter."

She could hear Carl Lundy's deep voice but couldn't make out the words.

Halor sat up straight. "What did you say?" He listened for a second, then held the phone at arm's length, staring at it. At the same moment, the lights went out, which was followed instantly by the sound of emergency sirens.

"We'll have to talk about this later," he said as the lights blinked back on. "But please give me a chance to explain." He stood up and put on his coat. Only her father was allowed to wear civilian clothing in Spell Realm. Even the guests seemed to accept it. He was Halor Mansing, the Founder. It made him stand out. It was a thrill for most people just to catch a glimpse of him.

Shara's anger drained away, because it was clear that whatever was happening was serious. She picked up the diary and nodded to her father. Halor had to pass by her, and he hesitated as if he wanted to hug her. She stiffened.

"Martinique would never have left you, Shara," he said quietly. "That's how I know."

He brushed past her and hurried out of the room.

Chapter 20

Since many visitors to Spell Realm are dressed as medieval war-riors or maidens and since most of them wield weapons, it might seem as if it would be difficult to keep things under control. Fortunately, our weapons are programmed to be harmless, to work only against other weapons or Flexstone creatures and to avoid living flesh.

I thought we'd have more problems than we've had, but it turns out that the folk who pretend at aggression are the least likely to commit real mayhem. Whether this is because of the catharsis from their play or because they are just happier people, I don't know. There are high expectations, however, and emotions sometimes do boil over, but so far, there has been nothing serious.

We have security personnel throughout the park, but they are well hidden among the role-players. They carry weapons designed to neu-tralize aggressors. So far, we've been lucky. Indeed, we've retrained most of our security people to be guides or role-players. After all, visi-tors need foils who are willing to pretend to be the villains, and to lose a fight.

But mostly, Spell Realm doesn't seem to be the kind of place where people come to cause trouble.

I can only hope this trend will continue forever.

— Martinique Mansing

The Mayerling sisters were waiting for Caleb on the steps of Castle La Magie. They didn't look happy.

"No luck?" he said, walking up to them.

"You're useless," Selene snapped. "We couldn't have done any worse on our own. Probably would've done better."

"I don't understand where Shara could be," Caleb objected. "She's not in her room or anywhere I've ever seen her. I don't think she's hiding…she doesn't know about us. I'm really at a loss."

"Shut up, both of you," Trina said. "There's something in the Mossy Forest I need to show you."

"Can't we call it a day?" Caleb was tired, and the forest was a long walk away. From her sisters' reactions, they didn't know what Trina was talking about either.

"You need to see it for yourself," she insisted. She led the way toward the tree-lined border of the tournament grounds. No one was playing games there. The pavilions were empty. People were scurrying about the park as if in a hurry. He hadn't seen that before—most people took their sweet time taking in all the sights when in Spell Realm.

"What's going on?" he asked.

"From what I understand," Selene said, "they're having some glitches. Things breaking down."

"Glitches?" Trina snorted. "I'll show you some glitches."

"What sorts of things breaking down?" Caleb asked.

Selene shrugged. "The dragon flew over while I was searching the tournament grounds. The damned thing set fire to one of the pavilions. I don't think *that* was supposed to happen. We need to execute this extraction as soon as possible."

"You don't have to convince me," Caleb said.

The forest was thick, and once under the massive boughs, it was as if they had entered a different, primeval world. These were real fir trees, imported fully grown with their massive roots encased in huge clods of earth. According to Caleb's research, they'd had to excavate down to bedrock, crushing stone as they went, to create a thick enough soil layer to support the forest.

There was a wide path through the woods. The tree trunks to either side were like the columns of a cathedral, the branches above a high wooden ceiling. Without meaning to, Marie and Selene, who'd been arguing about whether to go home, started talking in low voices.

Trina didn't join in the argument but marched down the center of the corridor until suddenly stopping. She turned and faced the others, extended one arm toward the left of the path, and pointed.

At first, all Caleb could see was a splash of red flowers in the thick carpet of bright green bushes.

No…there were no petals, no stalks, only the color red, some of it splashed onto the tree trunks. Trina waded into the underbrush, bent down, and pulled aside the greenery.

A body was exposed, wearing the green and brown of a ranger's costume. There were three legs among the tangle, and four arms; there were at least two victims here.

"I thought that such a thing was impossible," Marie said. "What sort of animal could do this?"

"None," Caleb said firmly. "There are no dangerous animals here. Every creature that has the appearance of being dangerous is a Flexstone creation, and as such, is programmed to be harmless."

"I don't think anything human or made by humans did this," Marie said. She looked around at the trees, trying to spot something. "Don't they have surveillance?"

"As far as I know, every inch of the park is covered by cameras except the private rooms," Caleb said. "This should have set off alarms."

"Are you deaf?" Selene snapped. "All I've been hearing for a day now is one alarm after another. Father taught us to pay attention to warnings. It's time to get out of here."

"What about our contract?" Marie asked. She didn't sound like she was disagreeing anymore, just trying to get the details right.

"We'll keep the advance," Selene said. "Our contract stipulates that if the situation is substantially different than we were told it would be, no money will be returned."

Caleb had finally had enough of these cold-blooded sisters. "There are two dead people lying here and all you can think about is your contract? We need to tell management."

The Mayerling sisters turned as one and examined him curiously. Then, as if by prearranged agreement, Marie spoke for the three of them. "It is none of our business. Let's go, girls. I've had enough of this place."

The underbrush rustled. Something was rapidly moving toward them. The sisters drew their daggers. Caleb unashamedly got behind them.

The sisters communicated without speaking. Selene and Marie nodded, while Trina raised her dagger above her head, holding the point between her thumb and forefinger. She squinted, moving the dagger back and forth as if measuring. Then, with a quick downward throw, the weapon flashed into the shadows.

Only a few feet away from them, the rustling stopped. An eerie screeching sound emerged from the underbrush, loud and high, before slowly descending to a last hiccupping cough.

Instead of wading into the undergrowth, the three sisters bent down and started cutting it away, inch by inch. Slowly, the thing's head was revealed, the dagger pinioning it to the ground like a stake. It was a snakelike creature with multiple legs, its head consisting of rows of teeth and two dark eyes that even in death radiated malevolence.

"All right, Caleb," Marie said. "You're the expert here. What sort of creature is this?"

"Whatever that is, it doesn't belong here," Caleb said.

"Is someone trying to sabotage the park?" Trina asked. "Besides us?"

Selene nodded "That...*thing* would certainly do it."

Caleb didn't have an answer. Something was going terribly wrong in Spell Realm, but he had no idea what was causing it.

Marie bent down and lifted a longsword from the undergrowth. She stabbed at the creature with the tip, which bent and then broke off. "Whoever those two dead people were, they didn't have a chance." She tossed the sword aside, then reached down and pulled the dagger from the creature. She wiped the blood off on a nearby tree trunk and handed it, hilt first, to Trina.

"Time to get out of here," she said. She started toward the castle, her two sisters following without a word. Caleb watched them, finally understanding that the sisters were a three-headed creature, not one individual.

Caleb no longer wanted to have anything to do with them. As they disappeared down the shadowy path, he turned around and went the opposite direction. Within a few hundred yards, the path ended at the side of a small pool.

He stopped and stared at the huge oak on the opposite bank of the pond.

He had the strangest feeling he'd been here before.

Even at midday, the ghosts of the two moons could be seen in the green sky.

The Sister Executioners gathered under the oak, arguing about what to do next. Calip heard the words "unicorn" and "impossible." The clear green pool reflected the color of the sky. They seemed to have completely forgotten about him. He started back up the path. No matter what happened next, he wasn't going to be part of it. He'd done his job, leading them to Lady Sharina. It wasn't his fault if they couldn't finish the task.

Besides, the surroundings were starting to freak him out. Everywhere he went seemed familiar, though he was certain he'd never been there before.

Calip felt relieved. He liked Lady Sharina, though he'd only spoken to her in passing. She'd recognized him just before the attack, he was sure of it. He would be as guilty in her eyes as the Sister Executioners were. It was time to go.

He hadn't gone more than a couple of steps before a stocky, dough-faced man came around the turn and stopped, staring at him curiously. At first, Calip thought he was a yeoman wearing a smock. Then he realized that it was a robe, and what he'd mistaken for dirt smudges were instead alchemist symbols.

Master Lumbli, the resident wizard of Castle La Magie, stepped forward, looking over Calip's shoulder. He frowned as he saw the three sisters, who were staring back at him.

"What are you doing here, young man?" the wizard asked.

"I was told that the unicorn sometimes shows up here."

"The unicorn?" Master Lumbli sounded dubious. "The Majestic Ultima is unlikely to show itself to the likes of you. You aren't a virgin, are you?"

Despite himself, Calip blushed. Truth was, before he'd become the Chance Knight, he hadn't been much of a prospect.

Since then, he'd distrusted the interest of the maidens who had put themselves forward.

"Hmmm," the wizard said, a slight smile on his face. "In any case, I'm looking for my young apprentice, Mill. You haven't seen him about, have you?"

"All I've seen are those three maidens under the oak."

"Curious," Master Lumbli said. "I've been out here a hundred times and never seen anyone but Lady Sharina. Now, suddenly, there's a throng."

As they were talking, the Sister Executioners approached. There was no other way back to the castle, though Calip wished they had waited until the wizard was gone. But they were on their best behavior, all smiles, even Selefor.

The wizard stepped aside to let them by. They began to pass, nodding pleasantly.

"Wait," Master Lumbli commanded. "I know you. What are the Sister Executioners doing in the province of Munsury? Has the Duke not banished you?"

As one, the sisters drew their daggers.

The wizard stepped backward into the undergrowth, almost losing his footing. He raised his arms and was surrounded by a glowing circle. Trinafor lunged, the point of her dagger aimed at his heart. The blade slid to the side with a juddering sound, as if ricocheting off of stone or glass.

Trinafor stepped back between her two sisters. They put their arms around each other's waists and chanted:

"Force of arms, troubled not,
Lift thy curse and smell the rot,
Into gizzards, the shine of blade,
Into gizzards, struck by maid."

Calip wanted to run, but the words pinned him in place. The three sisters rose from the ground, darkness growing around them until all he could see was the glow of their eyes and the gleam of their blades.

The light that circled Master Lumbli flickered and went out. He put out his hands, palms out, and fire flowed against the darkness of the three women. Neither side moved, locked together in a silent struggle.

Calip felt the hold on him being released, but when he tried to move, he fell backward. He stared up at the confrontation, feeling helpless.

The darkness expanded, and within it were three shards of light, pushing outward relentlessly toward the wizard. In response, his magical fire redoubled, and between the darkness and the blinding light, Calip could see nothing.

He wasn't sure how long he sat there in the mud before he noticed that the fire was starting to sputter, and with each blink of light, the daggers moved closer to the wizard.

And then a great wind arose, and both the darkness and the fire diminished in power. Calip looked up into the green skies and saw a dark shadow descending, and heard the thump of the dragon's wings as he slowed his plunge and hovered above them.

"Darke Dragon, protect the realm!" Master Lumbli cried.

The Sister Executioners abandoned their spell, floating to the ground. They turned and ran.

Something made Calip run in the opposite direction. The sisters nearly made it to the old oak before the dragon caught up to them. He reared back his head and breathed, and fire poured down on the sisters.

For a few moments, there was a dark bubble within the fire, but the blackness slowly shrank, and Calip heard a scream—Marifor, he thought. Then her two sisters joined her, and the scream became one voice, louder than the crackling dragonfire, at a pitch so high and desperate that Calip covered his ears.

The sisters separated, one of them slamming against the trunk of the tree and falling, another running into the reeds, setting them ablaze. The other two sister turned and ran for the pond, disappearing beneath the water.

The Darke Dragon continued to hover over them, pouring fire downward as the water boiled, until, with a final whump of his wings, he shot into the air and flew away.

The dragonfire continued to burn on the surface of the waters. The Sister Executioners did not reappear.

Chapter 21

My husband cares not for money or fame, which is one of the reasons I love him. So it is ironic that he has become paramount in both money and fame. He tries to forget this, I think, by working in his high tower.

He respects intelligence and education above all. If it was up to him, he wouldn't gift Shara anything but books. He lives in his mind, and he expects others to do so as well.

— Martinique Mansing

Shara followed her father, stunned and angry that he would walk out on her like that, as if she was just another employee to be dismissed. He walked fast, purposefully, looking neither right nor left. How many times, as a little girl, had she tried to keep up with her father when he was like this? It was as if he had forgotten she existed. He disappeared around the far corner of the hallway, and by the time she reached the corner, he was out of sight.

But she knew where he was going.

At least once a season, Spell Realm conducted a fire drill, mostly for the benefit of the park employees so that they'd know where to guide the guests in case of emergency. What *kind* of emergency was never specified, but any artificial habitation outside of Old Earth was in constant danger, despite the many safety redundancies.

Castle La Magie was a self-contained unit, capable of surviving for a long time without any outside help. With the power off everywhere but the hotel, the Personage-clad employees would by now be herding everyone to the safety of its shelter.

Halor would be heading for the grand ballroom, where the gathered guests would be waiting for instructions.

The hallways became more crowded the closer Shara got to the ballroom. The alarms were still blasting, so no one was trying to talk. Those employees who recognized her scrambled out of the way, prompting the guests under their stewardship to do the same. Ordinarily, Shara would have discouraged such special treatment, but this time she took full advantage of it.

The ballroom was packed, even though it was the off-season. She'd never seen it so full, even during the grand balls that she'd always thought were attended by most of the guests. Her father had made his way to the stage in front, where the orchestra usually played. He scrambled up onto the platform, where he was joined by some of his senior management.

The crowd quieted at the sight of Halor Mansing. He held up his hands. "Don't worry, we are safe. But if you don't mind, I'll wait until everyone arrives before addressing your concerns." He turned back to his staff while the murmur of the crowd once again grew.

Shara pushed her way to the stage. The steps were completely blocked, and no matter how she shoved, she couldn't get nearer. The crowd didn't know who she was. She looked up and saw that her father was standing right above her.

"Father!" she shouted several times before he looked down, frowning. He moved to the side of the stage and lifted her up with one sweeping motion. For a moment, they were close enough to hug, and Shara wasn't sure if she wanted that or not. Then the moment passed and he turned his back on her again.

She looked out over the growing mass of people. She recognized Personage-clad employees here and there, but nine out of ten were guests. At the far end of the ballroom, Millard entered, wearing his overalls.

Wait, is it Millard?

If his look of amazement at the size of the crowd hadn't given him away, the slight bow he gave her would have.

What is Mill doing here?

Halor was scanning the crowd. Shara was pretty sure that he

was looking for Carl Lundy. When her father suddenly relaxed, she knew Lundy must be approaching.

The big man pushed his way through the knot of people at the foot of the stairs and marched to his boss's side. They conferred for a short time, and Shara realized that far from being reassured, her father was alarmed. Perhaps no one else could have read the signs but her; it was the same hunching of the shoulders he gave whenever she questioned him. But whatever bad news he'd been given, by the time he turned around, he had that famous smile plastered on his face—the smile that was in all the pictures of him, the smile he never showed in private.

"I've been informed that we had a small increase in solar energy," he said, his voice deep and confident. "Nothing that Castle La Magie can't handle."

"Solar energy?" someone shouted. The voice was quavering, yet loud. Her father searched the crowd for the speaker and frowned when he saw who it was. "Do you mean radiation?"

The man was dressed in a jester's Personage, a doublet and hose patterned with red and black triangles and a tri-cornered hat with bells hanging down. The man appeared to be in his forties, but with the Personage, it was impossible to tell. He had the air of someone older, the sort of stillness that she'd noticed in Centennials.

"A slight increase in Fanchon Particles, Charles. There is nothing to be concerned about. Castle La Magie was built in the years following the Placers Planet incident. We are, if anything, overengineered."

Shara realized it was Charles Windford, who had lived in the park for as long as she could remember. A Perp. It was said he was the second-richest man alive.

The crowd began murmuring at that. It had been a mistake to mention the famous disaster: the Fanchon blast had evaporated the settlement's atmosphere, dooming everyone within.

In the century following the disaster, there had been mass hysteria over it. Colonization had slowed to a crawl, and what few new settlements were built were so expensive and constrictive that many had been abandoned.

Shara remembered that Charles Windford's fortune had

come from those years. Indeed, he'd been the one who'd sold the technology to keep the new settlements safe. He'd be one of the few people alive who remembered how afraid everyone had been back then. Slowly, public opinion had turned. Two neutron stars colliding was extremely rare. Not only that, but you had to be directly in the path of the resulting energy burst for it to be dangerous. The odds of that were so small that eventually everyone had realized that it was unlikely to ever happen again.

"I repeat, as long as we stay in the castle, we are safe," her father said. "I will, of course, not charge anyone for this inconvenience. If you wish to leave early, there will be no penalty."

"How kind of you," Windford said. "But I'm not sure that being on a ship is the best idea right now."

Halor frowned, wiping away the confidence of his smile. Shara had never seen him so distracted, so uncertain. He looked around the ballroom as if searching for an answer. Then he pointed into the crowd.

"Millard," he said. "Come on up here. Explain to these people why they don't have to worry."

Shara looked at Millard's twin, who had frozen in alarm. *Just turn around and leave,* she mentally urged him. Instead, the boy started forward, the crowd opening a path for him.

Uh oh. What's he going to say? That it's magic?

Now everyone was looking at him. Perhaps only she noticed Terry, and the real Millard behind him, in the ballroom's doorway. Terry's eyes widened and he pushed Millard out of sight.

Mill walked up onto the stage, seemingly unfazed. His "stepfather" draped his arm over his shoulder and gave him what was no doubt meant to be a confidence-boosting squeeze. Mill turned a little pale.

"He's just a boy," Charles Windford shouted. "What can he tell us?"

"Now, Charles. You of all people know how smart my step— my son is. He has made a special study of Placers Planet, haven't you Millard?"

Shara held her breath. She could see no way out of this.

"Yes, sir," the false Millard said. He faced the crowd, not looking intimidated in the slightest. "I will say this: If this was a true Fanchon burst, we'd already be dead."

Complete silence met this statement. It was so quiet, Shara could hear Charles Windford's chuckle. "How reassuring," the Perp said. "But the boy's got a point. Very well, Mansing, I'll sit tight. But if anything else happens, I want you to promise us that you'll tell us immediately."

"You have my word, Charles," Halor Mansing, founder of Spell Realm, said with all the confidence of his authority. The crowd began to disperse, excited that they were going to be given a few extra days in Spell Realm for free.

Shara quickly moved to Mill's side. "Come on, you," she hissed. "I don't know how you knew to say that, but let's not push our luck."

Chapter 22

The biggest argument Halor and I had during the planning for Spell Realm was how big to make it. We had found our world, and upon that world was a high, mostly flat plateau that was suitable for our park. I felt that we should enclose the entire area, whereas my husband felt that only a small portion was necessary.

Necessary? He and I had different ideas of what we were doing. I felt that Spell Realm should be as self-sufficient as possible. That we have enough acreage to grow crops, to feed livestock, to wander and get lost in. Forests must be deep and dark, rivers must flow freely, hills and dells must be natural and hard enough to reach that they feel newly discovered by all who explore them.

It is expensive, this I understand, and it has caused great stress on our marriage. If I would agree to license Flexstone, of course, all our financial worries would be over. So I am both the cause of the expense and the reason our revenue is short.

I believe that when Halor saw what we'd done, he agreed with me. Inside the protection of our shields, we are a real world, not just an illusion.

— Martinique Mansing

"**W**here's Millard?" Shara demanded the second she closed the door. It felt like a strange question, since her brain still insisted on seeing the person in front of her as her stepbrother instead of a stranger.

He glanced around her room with its pastel colors, frills, and round bed and gave her a sideways look. "It appears you are a princess in this world too, even if they don't call you that.

I was in a servant's quarters last night and it was nothing like this."

Shara felt uncomfortable, though she wasn't sure why. Mill was staring at her—not in the teasing way her stepbrother did, but as if he was assessing her. As if he was *admiring* her.

"I don't ask anyone to treat me differently," she said. "I work hard. I pull my own weight."

"I'm sure you believe that," he said. "But I've seen how others treat you; perhaps not with the obsequiousness of those in my world, but they show you deference even if you don't recognize it."

Shara knew he was right, though she purposely pretended the favoritism didn't exist. Sometimes she could almost convince herself. Mill went over to the bookcase and examined the titles. She was a little embarrassed, because she'd never bothered to replace her childhood favorites.

He pulled out a basic science book and held it up. "Mind if I take this?"

"You can learn a lot more from a tablet," she pointed out.

"Sadly, I do not have one."

"Oh!" she said. Of course, she had just assumed he wouldn't know how to use one. But she was beginning to wonder if there was anything this young man wasn't capable of. He was much more mature than her Millard, as if he'd endured hardships and dangers her brother could only imagine.

"Where's Millard?" she asked again.

Mill shrugged.

"We can't have the two of you running around at the same time," she said. It was really annoying that she was having to babysit this doppelgänger. What she wanted to do was be in the room below, reading her mother's diary. She could almost feel the pull of it.

"Why not tell the world?" Mill asked, sounding genuinely curious. "Is it not something remarkable? Isn't it something people should know?"

"If we were in your world, would you reveal it?" she countered.

He frowned. "No, I am not sure I would. Master Lumbli,

my…teacher, wouldn't approve. Nor do I wish to share. It is *my* magic."

"It doesn't matter," Shara said. "We have more important things to worry about."

"Yes, the Fanchon Particle burst. But I believe what I said was correct. If we were in the path of a burst, we'd be dead already."

"How do you know that?" she demanded. "Surely you don't have such a thing in your world."

"Not Fanchon Particles, perhaps, but we have something similar. We call them Spellshine, the spillover of dark magic from another land, adversely affecting our own. It is an easily understandable concept. I believe that there must be an analogy to just about everything in our two worlds; we simply use slightly different terminology. I did a little studying today in your library."

Shara sat on the edge of the bed, put her chin in hand, and examined this young man who looked and sounded like her stepbrother but also gave off a strangely disturbing aura.

He's as smart as Millard. I shouldn't underestimate him.

"As I said, it doesn't matter. We have bigger problems," she said. "I know my father. He's worried. I have a feeling that the danger to Spell Realm is worse than he is letting on."

"I believe it *does* matter," Mill said. "I don't think it is a coincidence that I have arrived here at this moment. My twin is obviously intelligent, though he seems hampered by these so-called scientific limitations. Perhaps with my help, the two of us can come up with a solution."

He came and sat next to her, and for a second, she thought he was going to put his hand on her thigh. She gave him a startled glance, but he didn't appear to notice her discomfort. He smiled, but it wasn't reassuring.

Someone pounded on the door. Mill jumped to his feet and assumed a fighting stance. His alarm was reassuring. Shara had begun to think nothing unnerved him.

"Sis! You in there?"

She rose calmly, went to the door, and opened it. Millard stomped into the room, followed less obstreperously by Terry.

Her stepbrother's gaze immediately fixated on his double. "You! What the hell do you think you're doing? You're lucky my father didn't figure you out."

"I had no choice," Mill said. "He called me up to the stage."

"Yeah, well, don't ever pretend to be me again."

"Gladly," Mill said. "Why don't we go see your father and Master Lundy right now? Let him know what you've done. Surely it is something to be proud of."

At that, the anger drained out of Millard.

"Better not," Terry warned. "Your father will ground you for life."

"I'm an adult," Millard grumbled. "I can do what I want."

"But not in Spell Realm," Terry pointed out. "Your father is king here."

Shara couldn't stand the bickering any longer. "Why are you guys even talking about it? None of that matters right now!"

Terry and Millard looked abashed, while Mill just looked amused. Millard turned to his double. "I left my tablet in my overalls," he said. "Hand it over."

Mill shrugged. "It fell out. I didn't pick it up. After all, it was of no use to me at the time."

Of all the things his double could have said, to Millard, this was apparently the most foreign. "You *dropped* it?"

"I'm sorry," Mill said, realizing that his twin was truly angry. "I didn't understand its importance."

Millard walked right up to his double and stood nose to nose with him. If they exchanged clothes, Shara wouldn't be able to tell them apart, at least in appearance. *And yet, there's something...*

"I don't like you," Millard growled. "I'm sending you back as soon as I can."

Shara couldn't help it. She started laughing, and Terry joined her.

Millard whirled on them, red-faced. "What?"

"He's you," Terry pointed out.

Millard stood still for a long moment, then, in a low voice, he said, "No. No, he isn't."

"It doesn't matter," Shara said, exasperated. Leave it to her brother to find a way to be competitive even with himself. "We need to figure out what's going on."

"Do we know the source of the Fanchon Particles?" Terry asked. "That might tell us something."

Millard threw up his arms, nearly shouting, "How should I know? I'm blind here!"

Shara thought for a second, then went over to her bedside table. She rummaged in the bottom drawer and finally brought out a large pink pad, decorated with glass jewels. A wave of nostalgia washed over her—she'd spent many a night scrolling through this old device. "Will this work?"

Millard snorted and turned away in disgust.

"Let me see it," Mill said. She handed it over, curious to see what he'd do with it. He turned it on, checked the energy level, and started whipping through the pages.

"How did you learn to do that?" Terry said.

"I spent the day in your castle library. It is the first thing I researched."

Shara was impressed. She'd grown up with this technology and it was still challenging sometimes, even to someone with her level of education. Mill seemed to be completely conversant with the workings of the device.

"It appears that Master Lundy has already pinpointed the location," he said.

"Really?" All of Millard's frustration disappeared. He looked over his twin's shoulder.

"How does that help us?" Terry asked.

"It does appear to be a Fanchon burst," Millard said. "I wonder if we are just catching the edges..." He started to turn away thoughtfully, then his eyes widened and his head jutted forward. "Magnify it, please."

Mill wasn't fazed in the slightest by the request. Moments later, both of them let out a small cry at exactly the same time.

"It's rotating!"

Shara wasn't sure which of them had spoken, but they both looked amazed.

"Is that possible?" Terry asked. "Has that ever happened before?"

"Not that I know of," Millard answered. "But then, there have been so few of these events observed, how would we know?"

"It's rotating toward us," Mill said. He swiped through a few pages, then nodded. "It appears that it is moving in our direction at a pace of about one degree per day. If the readings are right, we have twenty days before Castle La Magie's screens fail."

No one spoke for a few heartbeats, then Terry said, in a tone that sounded as if he'd just been handed a death sentence, "Does Mr. Lundy know?"

"I doubt it," Millard said. "The movement is very subtle. He'll figure it out, but maybe too late. He probably figures that we can wait it out, that we'll be safe inside the shields."

Shara said, "We have to warn him…and Father. We need to evacuate."

"It's too dangerous," Terry said. "The readings are already well into the red."

"Too dangerous compared to what?" Shara said. "Waiting until we get fried? There has to be a way to shield the ships until they're out of range."

"You could use the protection of the planet itself," Mill said.

Shara started toward the door, Terry at her side. But her stepbrother and his otherworld twin didn't budge. "Come on, you two. We've got to convince my father."

Millard shook his head. "Show Carl the rotation of the planet. He'll see it once it's pointed out. He'll know what to do."

"What about you?"

"I have an idea," Millard said. He looked toward Mill, who simply nodded, though neither of them had spoken to each other. Whatever it was, they'd both figured it out at the same time. Again.

Shara took the pink pad out of Millard's hand. She didn't doubt he could find another, more advanced device.

"Don't do anything stupid," she said. She took Terry's arm. "Let's go find my father."

Chapter 23

To the outside world, we appear to be the perfect couple, always smiling, always agreeing. Behind the scenes, Halor and I have argued over every little detail of Spell Realm. I get my way in the end, of course. The entire idea was mine, and Halor only went along with it to keep me happy.

"We are rich, my dear wife," he'll say to me. "But we aren't that rich."

It is a subtle reminder that we could easily be even wealthier if we simply licensed the formula for Flexstone and took royalties. It is said that Tesla once had a royalty rate per horsepower that would have made him the wealthiest man in history. He gave it up when the company licensing his AC power got in trouble.

Tesla died broke.

I simply don't trust the corporations of today, just as Tesla should not have trusted Westinghouse.

— Martinique Mansing

"Are you sure we should be leaving the two geniuses alone?" Terry asked. He'd seen the slightly maniacal, slightly distracted look Millard got when he was in the throes of another harebrained scheme. What was worse, he'd seen it in two pairs of eyes.

"What can they do?" Shara said. "Blow up the world?"

She led the way to an elevator that Terry hadn't even known existed. His stomach dropped as the elevator surged upward, a force of gravity Terry hadn't felt since arriving on a ship the year before. Neither of them spoke. The door opened on a huge office, and he realized that it could belong to only one person.

It was empty. Shara looked surprised. "I was so sure he'd retreat here," she muttered.

They went back the way they'd come, this time gravity seeming to disappear for a moment, and emerged on the landing outside Shara's room.

Her room had been a real eye-opener. He'd seen her current quarters, which were spare and utilitarian. But her childhood room had been fit for a princess.

Fit for the *princess.*

As they walked down the hallways, the only evidence of that young girl was the pink workpad she carried in her tanned hands. Her hair was short, and she never wore makeup that he'd ever seen. If you didn't know better, you'd have believed she really was the servant she pretended to be.

For the first time, he had a mental image of how she would look as one of the old-fashioned princesses who filled the park, with a flowing gown and makeup and an elaborate hairdo. It made his heart flip, for he realized that she would be more stunning even than those who hid behind Personages. Then he imagined her as one of the hags that the occasional guest chose as their costume, and he realized it wouldn't make any difference. He would recognize her in any shape or form. It was her presence he would know.

Carl Lundy was on the portico of Castle La Magie's main entrance, directing his crew. Terry felt a stab of guilt as he realized this is where he should have been. But when his boss glanced over at him, there was no sign of recrimination. Carl simply nodded.

That's when Terry saw something he'd only heard about and never expected to see.

King Halor stood in all his glory, his Personage fully engaged, with gleaming armor and a crown. In real life, Halor Mansing's beard was black peppered with gray, but in his park persona, both it and his long, flowing hair were pure silver.

Even more impressive, he was wielding a gleaming sword, its hilt made of a single ruby, its blade so bright that even in twilight, it was blinding. Anduren Dragonshorn. It was said that with this one tool, he could control all the creatures of Spell Realm.

There were many princes and princesses in Spell Realm, purchased for a price, but there was only one king. A wide circular space surrounded him, occupied only by Carl. Three or four maintenance workers were nearby, dressed in work clothes, not even bothering to turn on their costumes. Around them was crowd of guests, all watching the king's every move.

Halor and Carl were leaning over a large workpad, which had the same power over the park that Anduren Dragonshorn had, if in a more mundane form.

"Missing?" the king was saying, his deep baritone magnified by the Personage. Terry felt himself standing straighter. He glanced at Shara, who looked as dumbfounded as he was by her father's appearance—not just that he'd taken on the form of the king, but that he was out in public at all. Ever since Millard's mom had left, he'd been spending most of his time in the inner sanctum of his office.

"A young couple were out dragonling hunting. They aren't far, according to the sensors, just inside the forest," Carl explained.

"Why aren't they responding?"

"Well, that's the question, isn't it?" Carl said.

Terry watched the king's face to see what he made of Carl's impertinence. The king simply nodded. "They aren't moving," he said, his voice quiet.

"No, sir. They're not."

"Well, send someone out for them," Halor said. "How many radiation suits do we have?"

"More than the regulations demand, but far less than we need if we're going to venture outside Castle La Magie in any kind of numbers."

"That shouldn't be necessary," the king said. "We have more than enough supplies to last until help arrives." He surveyed the curious crowd, giving them a benevolent smile. He caught sight of his daughter and his smile grew broader.

Shara stepped into the empty circle, and the crowd's attention turned to her. "Father, I need to talk to you."

"Yes?"

"In private, if you don't mind."

He searched her face, and his smile dropped away. "Very well," he said, then turned to Carl. "Go retrieve the two guests."

"Yes, sir. I'll see to it myself."

"No," Shara said. "I need to talk to both of you."

Carl had already started to walk off, but at the tone in her voice, he turned around. His gaze passed over Terry, and for a second, Terry was certain his boss was going to assign the task to him. Then he barked, "Bates! Martini! We've got a couple of lost wanderers. Don some suits and go get them."

Two of the maintenance workers hurried off. The crowd opened up for King Halor and Carl Lundy, followed by Shara and Terry. They made their way to the small office off the entrance.

The king turned off his Personage, and Terry saw why he'd resorted to the disguise. Halor Mansing was shockingly haggard and thin. His hair wasn't gleaming silver but a patchy gray. The bags under his eyes seemed to be dragging down the rest of his face. "What's the problem, Shara?"

Shara brought up her pink workpad. There was a ghost of a smile on the king's face until he looked down at the graph. She quickly explained what Mill and Millard had told them.

"Is this true?" Halor asked.

"I didn't notice that the Fanchon Particles were increasing," Carl said. "My God, it's already getting worse just since the last time I checked. I don't understand. Fanchon bursts come fully formed...or so I thought. They don't increase in intensity over time."

"What do we do?" Halor asked grimly.

"We must evacuate immediately."

"I thought you said the radiation was too dangerous outside."

"It is!" Carl exclaimed. "In twenty years, a certain percentage of guests might come down with cancer. But according to this, if we stay, *all* of us will be dead in twenty days or less."

"Very well," King Halor said. He turned on his Personage, and his voice deepened. "Order the evacuation."

Chapter 24

We must endeavor never to show the science behind the magic. Flexstone will do most of what is needed, but there will need to be other devices. A power plant will be necessary, for instance. All must be hidden from view or disguised.

Digital illusion will need to be used for the costumes of both guests and park workers. I propose that we call these devices Personages, after the French word for "character."

The guests will be asked to give up all mechanical devices upon entering the park. We must be firm about this. Most will not want to give up their connection with their network, but we must insist. Why else are they here but to get away from it all?

Spell Realm must reside outside the real world, separate and alone. It must exist as if no other world exists, as if this is reality and everything else an illusion.

— Martinique Mansing

Mill almost followed Lady Sharina when she left the room with her servant.

No, not Sharina, he reminded himself. Her name is Shara. She is a completely different woman.

Yet the room was still filled with her presence. He looked around in wonder. Such luxury he'd rarely seen and had never known. Yet, if he understood correctly, Sharina had given up all this to be a commoner—or at least, to pretend to be one.

This must be what Lady Sharina's chambers look like, he thought. Of all the parallels between the two worlds, the castle was the most exact, even down to the name—Castle La Magie.

Every detail he had so far observed was the same.

But of course, he'd only accompanied Master Lumbli to the great castle a few times, and even then, he was barely allowed into the front entrance.

His double, Millard, was looking around the room with equal wonder. "This is a part of my sister I never knew. I've heard stories about what a princess she was, doted on by everyone. By the time I came along, she had rejected it all."

He turned back to Mill and gave him a nod.

"Am *I* thinking what *you* are thinking?" Mill asked. He looked into his twin's face, wondering how connected they really were. At first, he'd thought that they were exactly alike, apart from individual memories. Their abilities and personalities seemed to be very similar. But the more he was around his reflection, the more he realized that they thought about things differently.

Millard laughed. "I was about to say the same thing, but on this world, I'd ask, 'Are *you* thinking what *I'm* thinking?' But yes, I believe we must be. It makes the most sense. If the evacuation runs into trouble, it wouldn't be a bad idea to have a backup plan."

"I am not evacuating," Mill said firmly. "It would mean never returning to my own world."

"Oh…there's that," Millard said, as if it had never occurred to him. "Would that be so bad?"

"I am a wizard, not a… What do you call yourself?"

"I think of myself as an inventor."

"I am a wizard, not an inventor."

"I don't know," Millard mused. "You appear to be picking up the science pretty quickly."

"Yet I will always be behind, whereas in my own land, only my master is more advanced."

"A big fish in a small pond," Millard laughed.

"Indeed. That is a very apt description."

Millard nodded. "If nothing else, we can try to return you to your own home. We'll need to get to my work shed and to the prototype."

"What about the radiation?" Mill asked. It had alarmed him

to read of such a thing in the textbooks, but then again, if he simply thought of it as Spellshine, magic that had escaped a spell, it wasn't so foreign.

"The little time we are exposed between Castle La Magie and my shop shouldn't hurt us too much," Millard explained. "Once there, we'll be shielded enough. We can try to get a couple of radiation suits. I know where they're stored. That isn't the real problem, though. What's going to be hard is leaving without anyone stopping us."

"Is there not a secret way?" In his own land, Castle La Magie was riddled with such passages, known only to those in the Secret Societies, of which he was not yet an initiate.

"Well...there *are* the Vanishing Roads," Millard said thoughtfully. "I wonder if any are still operational."

"Vanishing Roads?"

"Magically hidden," Millard said with a grin.

Mill felt himself go cold. That had been the same tone he used when speaking to commoners about his spells. "Please do not talk down to me, Millard."

"Sorry," Millard said, not sounding sorry at all. "Vanishing Roads are service and maintenance paths and tunnels hidden from the public by digital shields—which I suspect are fried by now. But the designers of this park weren't above saving a little money by using natural barriers. We might be able to pick a path where we won't be observed."

"Lead the way," Mill said. "The longer we wait, the more dangerous it becomes. I want to go home."

Millard led his doppelgänger to the central Vanishing Road, which he knew was covered by a tunnel for about one fourth of the way, and then climbed a long ridgeline down the middle where they could hope to not be observed.

It was strange how his other self was already changing. He no longer gave everyone quizzical looks, but appeared to understand everything that was going on around him. He even seemed to understand some of the scientific concepts.

Along the route, Millard began to test his Other, filling in where there were knowledge gaps. It was quite satisfying to find that Mill was so smart, because it meant he was equally smart.

"How would you make your way unseen in your world?" he asked.

Mill looked down at his feet, then said, "I would cloak myself in a Spell of Distance."

"And what would that be?"

"People would see me, for it is impossible to disappear even in my world, but it would be as if they were seeing me from a vast distance."

"How do you go about that?"

"If I understand your physics correctly, it is the following formula." An equation came spilling off the twin's tongue, as if it was natural.

"Yes, but how do you do the *spell*? With words?"

Mill frowned. "Of course not. Words are just words. You must impose your will on the world. You reach out, as it were. Young wizards use hand and finger motions, but as you become more accustomed to it, your mind suffices—as long as the equation is correct in your mind."

"Show me," Millard said.

They stopped abruptly on the highest part of the ridge, which was visible for miles, but by now Millard didn't really care. It was doubtful anyone would be sent after them.

Mill showed him a complex series of hand motions, accented by finger positions. It all seemed silly and improbable, but then, there was no denying the existence of Millard's Other; therefore, the Otherworld—and magic—must also exist.

The wizard pointed the index and little fingers of each hand upward, palm out, the middle fingers and thumb folded down, and extended his arms out and downward.

Mill vanished.

Millard stumbled from sudden vertigo, almost toppling down the steep slope. He looked around in wonder, and in the corner of his eye, he caught a movement. Far away, beyond the castle, beyond the courtyards, was a small figure waving his hands.

Then Mill popped into view again, looking as amazed as Millard felt.

"It appears that some of the magic of your world remains," Millard said.

The wizard nodded. "I have sensed it, but never so strongly."

Millard was already mimicking what he'd seen his Other do. But no matter how accurately he positioned his hands and fingers, nothing happened.

"It is not the physical motions that create the spell," Mill said. "I have had years to learn the basics of magic. It's what's in the mind that counts."

Millard closed his eyes, and this time, as he moved his hands, he visualized the mathematical equation of optics, discovered so long ago by Galileo.

At Mill's startled shout, he opened his eyes. His twin was still standing a few feet away, but his eyes were unfocused, as if he was staring into the distance. Millard danced around his double, waving his arms energetically. Mill creased his brow as if disgusted. He reached out and grabbed Millard by the arm, and the spell was broken.

"Teach me more!" Millard exclaimed.

"Only if you teach me what you know in return," Mill replied.

They continued walking to the work shed, but neither was much aware of their surroundings. They excitedly exchanged formulas and spells, finding common ground almost immediately in most cases.

As they reached the end of the ridge, there was a steep path downward onto the flatland. The workshop was in sight. They broke off from their exchange to negotiate the hill, and as they did so, a sudden wind almost blew them off the path. Millard crouched down and got on all fours, and Mill followed his example.

"What is it?"

"Solar winds," Millard said. He felt the blood drain from his face, mirrored by Mill, who apparently understood radiation enough to know they were in trouble.

The wizard stood up and waved his arms over his head three times, and the wind stopped. Mill stood up gingerly, not quite trusting the sudden peace. "How did you do that?" he asked.

"Every spell leaves a lingering effect. The stronger the spell, the more powerful the residue. We call it Spellshine, and it is the most dangerous thing about magic. I used a spell to ward it off."

"And it worked," Millard mused. "Maybe we can use that."

But even as he said it, the wind returned. This time, they pushed on. It felt like all the soil so carefully brought from off-world to fill the rocky pinnacle of Spell Realm was blowing into their face. They stumbled on blindly, having no choice but to keep going. Twice, Millard saw his Other try to motion away the Spellshine, but to no effect.

Millard's outstretched hand struck something solid. He opened his eyes long enough to see that the doorway was to his left. He grabbed Mill's arm and scooted along the wall to the door.

He turned the knob and the door caught in the wind and flew open, almost striking them. They tumbled inside. Millard rose long enough to reach for the door and pull it shut.

They collapsed on the floor.

"Now what?" Mill asked.

Chapter 25

Of course, Spell Realm wouldn't have been possible without a suitable planet to experiment upon. Any planet with a strong magnetic core and shield was either already claimed or prohibitively expensive. Mere letters and numbers once identified the world now known as Spell Realm. It once had an atmosphere and water, the evidence being the deeply carved canyons where rivers once flowed. But its magnetic core had been too weak to keep the solar winds from scrubbing the planet clean.

Thus, it was ignored.

What my husband figured out was that the atmosphere of this planet had disappeared over eons. Any artificial atmosphere imposed on this high plateau would be barely touched in the hundreds, even thousands, of years that Spell Realm might conceivably exist. And by then, of course, science might have progressed to the point where it would no longer be a problem. In the time of any guest's visit, or indeed in their lifetime, the deterioration would be barely noticeable.

— Martinique Mansing

Terry was in awe, even though he knew the king's image was an illusion, a function of his Personage. He'd only been this close to Halor Mansing once before, the day he was hired. Since then, he'd only seen the great inventor from a distance. He was pretty sure that Shara and Millard didn't see him much more often than that. Shara was standing near her father, looking down at her pink workpad.

The Personage magnified the king's voice, making it deep and commanding.

"Please turn on your Personage," he told the gathered guests, "if you haven't already done so. It will give you some protection."

Many of those in the crowd, who had looked stressed and worried, suddenly became glittering, splendid versions of themselves. But the atmosphere of panic didn't quite dissipate. When Halor had called back the crowd to tell them to gather their belongings ("only what you can carry"), he hadn't bothered to try to reassure them. "We have no choice but to leave," he'd said, overriding all objections.

Only after most of the guests and workers were gone did he turn to Carl Lundy and whisper, "How many radiation suits do we have?"

"There are five listed in the manifest, milord."

"Only five?" Even the Personage couldn't hide the king's astonishment. "Five is a ridiculously small number."

"Your orders," Carl said.

The king nodded. "Five because the chances of anything happening were ridiculously small."

"Five suits," Carl repeated. "Three of which we can't find. We've had few occasions to leave the boundaries of Spell Realm."

"We shall need to reach the ships swiftly, to expose our guests as little as possible," Halor said. "How many buses do we have?"

"None operational, milord," Carl said. "The burst fried all the wiring. All of the vehicles have stopped working."

The king was silent at this.

"We can hook up the horses to the carriages," Carl suggested. "With our current capacity, it shouldn't take more than five trips to ferry our guests out to the ships."

"Use the radiation suits to harness the horses and get everything ready," Halor commanded. "Once we start, we need to finish as quickly as possible."

"Yes, milord," Carl said.

"Stop that," the king said.

"Milord?"

"Quit calling me that. I am not a king. We are all equal before the storm."

"If you say so, sir," Carl said, not sounding convinced.

"I'd like to volunteer," Terry said, stepping forward.

Carl smiled. "Oh, you think it's a matter of volunteering, do you?"

Terry felt himself flush, wondered how much his Personage hid it.

"I'd like to help too," Shara said, stepping to his side.

"Absolutely not," her father said. Shara froze for a moment at his commanding tone, then shook it off. "Father, we are all equal before the storm. Remember?"

"If she's wearing a suit, sir," Carl said, "she'll be safer than the rest of us. And she's better with the horses than anyone I know."

As they spoke, the first guests were returning to the ballroom, many of them bringing cartloads of luggage. A look of imperial exasperation crossed the king's face.

"Hurry, then," he said to Terry and Shara. "Shara, you will only be allowed to come with me if you wear one of the radiation suits."

"But Father..."

"No buts. Wear it or remain behind."

He turned his back on them and spoke to the crowd. "Leave everything but what you can carry in one pack. I promise that I will reimburse you for any lost possessions."

Terry caught the worried look on Shara's face. "Great. No doubt everyone is leaving behind precious jewelry worth a fortune—at least, that's what they'll claim." She turned to Terry and shook it off. "Whatever...we can afford it. Let's go."

Carl led them to the two radiation suits. Both of them were small, as if made for a child or a young teen. Shara struggled to get into the biggest one, which was stiff from disuse. It was bright yellow and bulky, but after a few seconds, it molded to her body. When she was done, she lifted the other suit thoughtfully.

"There is Flexstone in these suits," she said.

The stables were only a couple of hundred yards out back of Castle La Magie. Carl slapped them on the backs and sent them on their way. A strong wind struck them as soon as they opened the doors. Dust pattered against the helmets and faceplates of the radiation suits. Shara turned on her helmet lights and pushed forward against the wind. They could see only a few feet in front of them for most of the way, and then, a few yards from the stables, the wind died down.

The horses were milling about, over forty of them, some of them retired from active duty and living out their lives in peace. The five working carriages were parked alongside the barns. Each of them normally carried twenty passengers, those who were too elderly or too disabled to walk around the park.

"These will carry at least thirty-five people each," Shara said, gazing on them with a calculating look. "Maybe more. But I don't see how they can provide much protection."

The carriages were usually open, but Terry knew that they had the capacity to be enclosed. In the first few decades of the park, Martinique Mansing had insisted that Spell Realm have the same atmospheric conditions as a real world; rain, wind, and even snow. After her disappearance, Spell Realm had become perpetually sunny.

"The sides close up," Terry said.

"But won't Fanchon Particles go right through them?"

"They were built when the regulations generated by the Placers Planet disaster were still being imposed."

Shara nodded. "I'm sure my father would have insisted even if it wasn't legally required. Very well. I believe each carriage will need at least six horses. Follow my lead, Terry."

Terry nodded and gulped. Apparently she knew how inept he was with horses. Stableboy had been his first job, until Carl Lundy had come along to save him. He didn't trust the animals; their beady eyes always seem to be measuring him for weakness. He could never get them to do what he wanted them to do.

Shara, on the other hand, loved the creatures. The first time he saw her was as she galloped by the stables, her long hair flowing. (She'd still been a princess then, and far out of his reach. But his love for her had begun at that moment.)

She took the lead, so the horses were compliant. They quickly harnessed six horses to the first carriage. As Terry was tying the last of the straps, Shara went off and came back with a solitary saddled horse. Terry recognized it as the horse she always rode, a beautiful buckskin stallion with a dark mane and tail. She tied the reins to the back of the carriage. "Drive to the castle, then ride back on Sam. I'll have the next vehicle done by then."

He almost objected, then realized that she'd probably be almost as fast without his "help" as she was with it.

He drove the carriage around to the front of the hotel. The wide steps were full of people, all jostling to get in front. King Halor was trying to control the mob, and as soon as Terry pulled up, a couple with three young children boarded, followed by another young family.

Terry nodded to his boss, mounted Sam, and headed back.

Shara had harnessed a team to a second wagon and was at work on a third. They didn't speak as he quickly tied the buckskin to the back of the second carriage and drove off.

By the time he returned from delivering the third vehicle, Shara had finished the fourth and fifth wagons, and had also saddled the remaining horses and tied each one to the back of a carriage.

This time, they drove back together.

Terry expected Halor and Carl to have already started conveying the guests to the ships, but the carriages were lined up, filled to the brim, with at least forty people per vehicle and maybe more. The steps were nearly empty. It was only going to take a couple of trips to get them all aboard the ships.

Halor smiled when he saw the saddled horses and quickly went to one of them and mounted.

Shara rode to his side, looking like an alien in her yellow suit. "Father, you are too exposed."

"I'm rich, remember?" Halor said in a booming voice that everyone could hear. "I can pay for gene therapy that will heal any damage. Indeed, I intend to pay for everyone!"

There was a moment of silence, and then cheers erupted, magnified by the enclosed spaces within the carriages. "Long live the king!" someone shouted. Several people emerged from the crowd, dressed as knights, with armor and swords. They mounted the other saddled horses.

"We will return shortly," the king said to those who were left. "You will be safe within Castle La Magie." He spurred his horse to the front of the line, followed by the other riders, including Shara and Terry.

He waved his arm and pointed forward. Slowly, lumbering, the overcrowded carriages followed him.

Chapter 26

I will insist that the spaceport be outside Spell Realm's shield walls. We will allow a narrow tunnel for the guests to be transported inside, just large enough to fit a carriage pulled by horses. All technological devices brought by guests will be blocked once inside, including any implants.

We will, of course, have a separate entrance for such supplies as we must import. This haven will be on the far side of Spell Realm, out of sight and out of reach of visitors. I hope that in time, we will have no need of outside resources, though Halor is convinced that will never happen.

When we first thought of Spell Realm, we thought the idea would attract financing through normal channels, but the financiers saw problems with our business model. Perhaps the biggest problem, as they saw it, was Spell Realm's isolation. They simply could not conceive of a place where they could not promote or advertise, where the customers would be alone, interacting with others only in person.

But a fantasy that can be punctured by reality is no fantasy at all.

— Martinique Mansing

The workshop rattled in the wind, with sharp bangs as things plucked from the ground were hurled against the metal sidings. Somewhere in that dust storm was the contraption that had brought Mill to this world. It had been open along the sides, he remembered, with wires and all kinds of hardware that Mill hadn't been able to make sense of.

"The Entangler won't work with Fanchon Particles blasting it," Millard said.

"What do we do?" Mill asked his double.

"The workshop is too small to contain the Entangler," Millard said, frowning. "That's why it's outside."

"Do you think the awning is still over it?"

"I doubt it. Don't you?"

The shed shook violently, seeming to shift around them. Mill didn't bother to answer.

"We'll need to take it inside Castle La Magie's shields," Millard said.

"Do you have a…" Mill struggled to remember the name of the conveyance that carried heavy material on this world. "…a truck?"

"Doesn't matter. I doubt they're working. But I do have a trailer we can winch it onto. The stables aren't far away. We'll get a team of horses."

Horses also existed on Mill's world, and he was well acquainted with them.

It became quiet outside. Mill went to the door and cautiously opened it. He let go of it, expecting it to catch in the wind and fly open, but the door remained open only a few inches. He pushed it the rest of the way open and went outside.

They could now see all the way to Castle La Magie, which glowed in the distance. Only a few yards away in the courtyard, the Entangler still stood upright. It had withstood the winds, probably because it was so heavy. The top plate had blown off, and there were loose wires everywhere and sand was caked into every cavity, but it was, amazingly, intact.

Millard went to the machine and started poking around with a sharp tool. Dust streamed down the side, but where he worked, shiny metal surfaces were revealed.

"My shop teacher taught me to use heavy solder if I could afford it. I think this can all be repaired." He looked up at the sky, which was slate gray with streaks of red, as if there was fire behind the clouds. "There's a flat cart in back that I used to carry parts out here. Help me pull it around."

The trailer was open and small, with two fat tires. Nevertheless, it was hard to budge. Once they got it rolling, they managed to maneuver it beside the Entangler, which looked too big for it. Millard measured it, detached the two sides of the trailer and nodded in satisfaction to himself.

"How do we get it on?" Mill asked. He couldn't help but think of spells he'd use on his own world, but when he reached for them here, nothing happened. Whatever magic still lingered in this world came and went unreliably.

"I think I have some block and tackle in the shed," Millard said. He looked up at the skeleton of the awning. The roof was gone, but the overhead struts were still there. He left and came back dragging a heavy chain. "Bring the pulleys," he told Mill.

Mill realized that the books he'd read had been too advanced for this kind of basic mechanics, but he guessed that the heavy metal tear-shaped tools near the doorway were what Millard was looking for. He could only lift one at a time. He took the first one to his double, who grabbed it without comment and started sliding the chain into it.

Mill went back for the others. By the time Millard was done, he had strung the chain over the metal frameworks and was wrapping the other end around the top of the Entangler.

It is simply a mechanical representation of the Fulcruming spell, Mill realized. *How crude.* In his own world, he could do the same thing with a simple thought.

As they started to pull on the chain, the Entangler lifted from the ground with amazing ease. Millard went over to steady the machine, leaving the wizard to lift it all by himself, with barely a strain.

"How simple," he said aloud.

"Indeed," Millard says. "Yet effective. It's just leverage."

Mill stopped pulling, dumbstruck. With such a device, any commoner in his world could do what required an apprentice wizard years and years of training to accomplish. He began to see how all people could be lifted, as if by a fulcrum; everyone could build and create without recourse to wizards or monarchs.

Of course, the Secret Societies would stop the spreading of such knowledge. In Munsury, wizards were as powerful as monarchs, and indeed sometimes became royalty in their own right. Others, like his Master Lumbli, preferred to be the power behind the throne, but to enjoy all the privileges and luxuries of the highest nobility.

I will have a choice, Mill thought, to give such knowledge to all, or to keep it to myself and retain my status.

They lowered the Entangler onto the cart. Millard tested the sides and found that he could barely close and latch them. He removed the chains, and they secured the machine to the cart. Its fat wheels sank into the dust.

"A couple of horses will do the job," Millard said, sounding satisfied. "Let's go."

Mill followed, eager to once again engage in an activity he knew well. Horses he understood, since they were the usual form of transportation in Munsury. As they approached the stables, Millard suddenly started running. He threw open the doors and cursed.

"Where did they all go?" he shouted.

They both turned toward Castle La Magie. Large carriages were drawn up in front of the hotel steps.

"Damn them," Millard said. "Did they have to take them all?"

There was a rustle from the darkness at the end of the stable, and they both turned in anticipation.

Horny the unicorn ambled toward them, seeming eager and happy, but halfway there, he stumbled, barely staying upright.

"The stable walls must have protected him," Millard said. "Perhaps…" He approached Horny, put his hand on the horn, pulled down the mechanical creature's head, opened something at the back of the neck, and looked in. "If we can protect his operating system, we might be able to make old Horny last long enough."

"Is the creature strong enough?" Mill asked.

Millard snorted. "He's worth ten horses…when he's working correctly. My stepfather built these creatures to last."

"But once he's outside, won't the Spellshine destroy him?"

Millard went to the corner of the shed and started grabbing stuff from a pile, throwing most of it over his shoulder in exasperation. Finally, he pulled out a thick blanket and shook the dust off it. "Lead-lined. It might buy us enough time."

He wrapped the blanket around Horny's head, leaving only his eyes and horn exposed. They quickly constructed a makeshift harness, which Horny readily accepted. Despite knowing that the unicorn wasn't real, Mill couldn't help but perceive emotions in the thing. He appeared to be grateful to the humans for paying attention to him.

The wind started to pick up outside the stable again. They opened the door and led Horny out. The unicorn paused. Millard slapped the creature's flank and yelled, "Haw!" and the unicorn jerked forward.

They made it back to the workshop just as the wind reached a crescendo. Millard and Mill hesitated and looked at each other, and neither had to speak. There was no time to take shelter.

They managed to hook up the cart to Horny's harness, and once again Millard slapped the creature's flank and shouted wordless encouragement. Horny strained for a few moments, then the tires pulled out of the dust with a dull pop and the cart trundled forward noisily, the Entangler swaying alarmingly atop it.

Mill could barely catch his breath the first half of the trip back to Castle La Magie, both because the dust was choking and also because it seemed like every step would be the last, for both Horny and the cart. Horny's movements became jerky, and one of the straps around his neck broke and the mechanical unicorn started veering off to the left of the path. Millard grabbed the reins and pulled his head in the right direction.

The shield around Castle La Magie was visible because the wind-blown dust dropped to the ground as it struck the force field, like rain hitting a window. Not more than fifty feet away from its beckoning safety, Horny jerked forward one more time and froze.

Millard and Mill had been pushing against the back of the cart, and now they staggered, falling to their knees. Mill couldn't even stand, he was so winded. His heart was beating so fast that the individual beats ran together. He hadn't realized how hard he was laboring.

Millard stood up and looked toward the shield. It was so

tantalizingly close, and yet it might as well have been a hundred miles away.

"They will return soon with the horses," Mill said. Clustered on the steps were several dozen guests and piles of luggage. Obviously, they hadn't been able to evacuate everyone on the first trip.

"It'll be too late," Millard said. "It might already be too late. The circuits are being fried with every second that passes."

A little girl broke away from her father. "Look!" she cried. "A unicorn!"

She almost made it to the shield before her father caught up to her and snatched her into his arms. He was a burly man; his Personage couldn't quite conceal his girth. It gave Millard an idea.

"Sir!" he shouted, walking toward the crowd. "I need your assistance, as well as four or five more of you."

The big man was dressed as a knight, but if Mill had encountered him on his own world, he would have guessed him to be a blacksmith or wagon master. He stared at Millard as if he was looking at a fantasy creature as unique as the unicorn.

"I'm not going out there," he said. A few of the other guests had started to move forward, but at this, they hesitated.

"Maybe we should help them, Winston," one of them said.

"I don't trust you people," Winston said. "Just because High Lord Almighty Halor Mansing says he'll pay for damage doesn't mean he will."

"I must insist," Millard said. "It is for your own good."

"You are not in charge of me, little lordling," Winston said. "The fantasy is wearing thin around here."

Millard looked like he was going to face off against the big man, which would have been funny if it wasn't so alarming. Mill pulled his double away.

They returned to the cart, where Horny still stood frozen, his right front leg lifted as if ready to step forward. Millard kicked at one of his back legs. "Worthless piece of junk!"

It seemed to Mill that there was still life in the creature's black, limpid eyes, that he could read shame and fear underneath.

"I believe there is magic in this creature," he said.

"What's that?"

"There is something in this creature's being, as with many of the objects in this world, that seems to have an element of magic."

"We call it Flexstone," Millard said gloomily. "Nothing magical about it."

Mill waved a Spell of Revealment, and sure enough, he could see the glow of magic within the unicorn's body.

Millard read something in his expression. "You really think so? You know, I've always wondered…"

But Mill was already forming a Spell of Animation. The unicorn's hoof came down, and he pranced sideways a couple of steps, as if in surprise. It was Horny, but sleeker, bigger, and more colorful. His horn narrowed and elongated as they watched, and the creature jerked forward as if springing for freedom.

The cart lurched, and the Entangler swayed alarmingly. The unicorn pulled against the harness, and for a second, it appeared he would break his bonds, but instead, the cart rolled forward and Mill had to hurry to catch up.

By the time the unicorn and the cart were inside the shield, any semblance to Horny was gone. This was a real unicorn, the same creature Mill had tracked for months in his own world, rarely catching a glimpse of him.

The unicorn reared upward. The straps of his harness disappeared and the unicorn broke away, his ivory hoofs clattering on the stone steps.

The little girl squealed in delight and rushed toward the creature. He lowered his head, splaying his front legs, ready to defend himself. Out of nowhere, the girl's father was there. The unicorn lunged forward, impaling the large man in the shoulder, and slung him effortlessly into the castle wall.

His daughter screamed and the rest of the crowd froze.

Mill discontinued the spell, but the unicorn was undiminished. He turned his head and glared at Mill, tossing his shimmering mane. There was no sign of the old Horny. With a last whinny, a musical note never before sounded upon this world, the unicorn turned and sprinted into the dust outside the shield and disappeared.

Two spells in a row were too much for Mill; his energy was gone. His legs went out from under him, and he plopped down cross-legged on the steps, head down, staring at his lap. When he raised his head again, Millard was standing near the Entangler, prodding its wires as if nothing unusual had happened.

Chapter 27

Against my better judgment, we have used Flexstone in Spell Realm much more than I wanted to. Originally, I'd hoped to keep it limited to the fantastical creatures and, of course, Castle La Magie.

But eventually I realized that the upkeep of the roads and other infrastructure of the park was going to be prohibitively expensive. By using Flexstone everywhere we could, our park became self-repairing and self-sustaining.

But I fear sometimes that this technology will leak to the outside world.

I've never told my husband of my doubts. If it was up to him, he'd give Flexstone to everyone who asked, freely and without expectation of return. I know that I am considered a dragon lady for keeping the technology to ourselves.

But think what would happen if everyone could use Flexstone anytime they wanted, for any purpose. If ever there was an emergency, if ever the invention stopped working for whatever reason, humanity would be helpless. Of course, the same thing can be said of all our technology. Without it, we would fall back into primitive ways. We would probably survive without most inventions. But if nanotechnology were used for every purpose, I doubt we would survive its loss.

— Martinique Mansing

Castle La Magie's lights were still illuminating the way when they found themselves in trouble. For the first time in her life, Shara was discovering what it was like to live in a world without the magic of Flexstone. The roads, which were designed to repair themselves, were quickly rutted by the first two wagons, so that by the time the fifth wagon came along, the wheels were scraping against the sides of the furrows, jerking the passengers violently from side to side.

The king rode in the lead, unaware of what was happening in the back of the caravan. Shara thought of riding forward to tell him, then decided there was no point. Her father couldn't do anything about it.

Terry rode at her side. Despite having once been a stableboy, he was awkward in the saddle, and his horse could sense it. She occasionally tried to have her own head, ambling away from the path. He kicked the recalcitrant mare in the sides and pulled mightily on the reins, but it was only when Shara rode to his side and guided him back to the trail that the horse cooperated.

"Miserable animals," Terry grunted.

Shara smiled. His ineptness with horses endeared him to her. Many a young man had tried to impress her with his horsemanship, but it rarely had anything to do with their character. Terry was honest to a fault, never playing games with her, and that was worth any number of spoiled young men with their father's fortunes.

Something wet struck her cheek, and she looked toward the carriage in front of her, wondering if one of the passengers had spilled a drink. Then another drop hit her face, and another, and then it really started raining.

The carriages stopped. None of the drivers would have ever seen rain in Spell Realm. Shara knew from reading her mother's diary that the park had originally included all kinds of weather, including rain and snow, but those mechanisms had been turned off decades ago in favor of perpetual sunshine.

No one had complained.

But whatever system had been used to deliver rain hadn't disappeared. Instead, it must have been storing up water all this time. This wasn't rain in the sense of individual raindrops. It was more as if a giant pail of water was being dumped on their heads, and it continued to pour as if bottomless. The rutted tracks quickly became a quagmire. The fifth wagon stalled first, then the fourth wagon.

"Tell them not to stop!" Shara shouted to Terry when she

realized the lead wagons were slowing. She guessed that if they stopped now, they'd never get the wagons going again. Terry spurred his horse, and for once, the mount responded.

Shara rode to the fourth carriage and saw that its wheels were embedded in mud up to the axles.

"The strongest must get off and push!" she shouted to its passengers.

No one budged. Then, from the very center, the stooped form of Charles Windford emerged. He walked to the carriage steps and gingerly, holding tight to the bannisters, lowered himself into the mud.

One by one, others followed, too embarrassed to let the old man be the only volunteer. They pushed against the back of the carriage as the driver whipped the horses, who reared and pulled in shock, for none of them had ever been treated that way before.

The wagon lurched forward, and mud flew into the air from the wheels, coating the pushing passengers.

"Don't stop!" Shara shouted to the driver as the wagon broke free and started rolling forward.

The passengers on foot struggled to catch up, but in the end, most of them managed to hop on. The passengers in the last wagon didn't need any urging; the strongest of them were already pushing it. The wagon popped loose from the mud with a suction sound that could be heard over the slapping rain.

Shara rode to the front of the caravan to urge her father to hurry. If anything stopped them now, she doubted they'd ever extricate themselves.

Her horse strained to scramble up a slope, a hillside Shara couldn't remember ever climbing—and she'd traveled this road more times than she could count. One summer, she'd ridden to the port almost every day, waiting for a pen pal from a world far away, disappointed every time, for in the end, despite promising to visit, the distant friend had never arrived.

But the terrain was now unrecognizable. Without Flexstone maintaining the road, without blue skies and sunshine, the course was suddenly windy and steep and forbidding. The dust storms that had arisen earlier that day combined with the torrent to create rivulets of muddy water that threatened to turn into mini-flash floods.

Shara surmounted the hill. At the base of the far slope, one of the carriages was turned on its side, and people were working frantically to rescue the trapped passengers. The spaceport was now in sight, the tops of the ships poking over the trees.

Her father was on his horse, gesticulating as he issued instructions. Terry was next to him, mimicking his boss's motions, and Shara could hear his stronger voice.

The port had been built on a smaller flat island outside Spell Realm, connected to the mainland by a bridge.

Shara tried to make sense of what she was seeing. Rushing waters filled the deep canyon, and there was no sign of the bridge. How could the water have risen so high? It was as if they were on an alien world, unlike the neat and orderly Spell Realm she'd always known. This was the kind of thing her mother would have liked; the danger, the unpredictability.

Halor rode to the side of the gorge, looked into it, then slumped in his saddle, seemingly defeated. Then he straightened and raised his sword high. Anduren Dragonshorn glowed in the dim light, as if it was gathering all the illumination available.

The overturned carriage had been pushed back onto four wheels, and the passengers were getting back on. Everyone stopped what they were doing to watch. From the cliff, a bulge appeared, pushing into the torrent. The sword Anduren flashed a bright red and the bulge turned into a platform that extended halfway across the gap, the rushing waters spilling beneath it. The king spurred his horse onto the platform, which extended before him.

It seemed to Shara that it became darker around her, that the only thing visible was her father, his armor and sword lit from within. He seemed taller, and his helmet, which had been a simple one, appeared to grow jewel-tipped spikes. The horse, which she'd thought was a dappled brown, was now an ebony black, as dark as the night.

The sword looked longer, wider, and though there was no way she could have known this, sharper and deadlier. Halor

Mansing was no mere king, he was a sorcerer king with all the powers of magic at his bidding. He was the master of Spell Realm, all the way down to the soil beneath their feet.

The bridge continued to grow and widen. The original bridge had been utilitarian. This earthen viaduct was even cruder, but it seemed to Shara that she could see a new bridge overlaid across the old; high and slender, as clear as glass, with towers on both ends.

Lightning struck the plateau on the other side of the gorge. Shara had only read of lightning, but when it was followed by a thunderous roar, she realized what it was.

The horizon shimmered, and then the image of the fairy bridge shattered, leaving only the dirt bridge beneath. Spell Realm stopped at the end of the bridge, and the bare rock on which the span was anchored splintered and broke away.

Halor Mansing shrank to a mere human, astride an unremarkable brown horse. Only his sword kept any semblance of power. He pointed Anduren at what was left of the bridge, the sword flashing so brightly that Shara shielded her eyes. For a moment, the bridge held.

And then it broke beneath the horse's hooves, and her father plunged into the churning waters. He surfaced just once, his sword held high, and then disappeared into the inky blackness.

Shara cried out and spurred her horse toward the gorge. Somehow, Terry outrode her, cutting her off. She jumped off her mount and rushed to the bank. Terry flung himself off his horse, ran after her, slid to a stop beside her, and nearly tumbled into the maelstrom. She reached out and grabbed him. A moment before, Shara had been ready to jump in after her father, but while saving Terry, reason returned and she understood that it was hopeless.

Her voice sounded unbelieving to her own ears. "He's gone."

Chapter 28

Without the dragon, Spell Realm is just another amusement park. Oh, the fantastical creatures are a little more convincing, the unicorn is a delight, the griffins and wyverns impressive, but it is the dragon people come to see.

Against my better judgment (I know that I often say that, but it has been a constant battle between my vision of what Spell Realm could be and the necessities of economic reality), I allowed a naming contest for the dragon, and as I feared, the names submitted were kitschy and precious. Every dragon name in popular culture was suggested, going back as far as Old Earth stories of Puff and Smaug.

I wouldn't have it.

In the end, someone from far away finally came up with the name I wanted all along (I don't know, I may have hinted at it), a name that was anything but lovable, that hinted of gloom and danger.

Darke. (I compromised on allowing the "e"; otherwise, I doubt I could have ramrodded the name through the contest committee.) I made sure Darke's design wasn't cute and cuddly. I made sure that he breathed fire, and that his fangs and talons were sharp.

Halor complains daily about our insurance rates, but to me it is a fair price to pay for making our fantasy real.

— Martinique Mansing

They straggled back to Castle La Magie. Terry took the lead at first, urging everyone to turn around and start back. Shara was in shock. The larger-than-life figure who was her father was gone, and it hit her harder than she would have ever expected. He had been a distant presence in most of her life, but now memories of gentler times flooded through her and her tears overflowed.

When the carriages started floundering, she found the present emergency an escape from those painful remembrances. The drivers whipped the horses relentlessly, but there was nothing the animals could do to free the wheels from the cloying mud.

"Enough," she shouted, her voice harsh and low. She heard echoes of her father's tone in those words, and it gave her a moment's pause. Then she realized that it was exactly what was needed. "Dismount! Leave your luggage. We must quickly return to Castle La Magie!"

What she didn't say, but which most of them would realize, was that invisible Fanchon Particles were flowing through their bodies, washing through vulnerable flesh and cells and genes. Every minute they spent exposed was equal to a lifetime of normal radiation. Staying in the carriages would protect them for a short time, but only Castle La Magie offered any real protection.

If only for a few more days.

Shara felt guilty for wearing the radiation suit, and she almost stripped it off and handed it to one of the others, but she knew that would take up too much needed time. Instead, she made sure that she was last in line. She could tell from Terry's expression that he understood her intentions, and he joined her.

They helped the stragglers as best they could, especially the elderly and the young, and especially those children too big to carry for long but too young to move fast. Shara lifted one small child into the saddle and led her horse. Terry walked beside her, having done the same. The damage being done to all of them would be irrevocable if they couldn't make it to the ships and get to hospitals off world. Already her mind was turning to that problem.

The rain was a constant spray that flew into their faces, as harsh as sand. The ground started to congeal, the mud thickening. The roads were so rutted that most of the refugees had spread out from them and were making their way across the open landscape.

Castle La Magie beckoned in the distance. Without those bright lights and the knowledge of the dry warmth that awaited them, many might have given up. But finally, the last hundred yards came into view. It looked like miles.

Shouts reached them, and Shara saw people clustered on the castle steps, waving encouragement. A few brave souls rushed out from behind the shield, snatching up the children and helping the older people. Shara looked up at the young child in the saddle. She couldn't determine their gender. "Hold on tight, sweetie." She slapped the horse's rump and he shot forward, the child almost tumbling off, and trotted toward the lights.

Terry did the same with his charge. They exchanged glances, and Shara, overwhelmed by sorrow and exhaustion, resisted the urge to fall into his arms. She didn't have that luxury. Seconds counted.

She trotted toward the castle with the last of her strength.

It shouldn't have been possible for her to know when she passed within the protection of the shield, but nevertheless, she felt it. A warm sensation came over her, as if her body had been falling apart and now solidified.

She dropped to her knees, and then lay on her back, closing her eyes, shutting out all thoughts. Grief overwhelmed her again, and she heard herself let out a cry. A warm hand brushed her forehead, and she opened her eyes to see Terry sitting beside her with a concerned expression. Standing behind him was Millard…and then the other Millard came into view, and the sight was so strange that she found herself laughing through her tears.

"Where's Halor?" her brother asked. "Where's…Father?"

The hysterical laughter froze in her throat. She couldn't answer.

"He's gone, son," Carl Lundy said gently.

He looked from Millard to Mill as if uncertain which to address. Mill put his arm around his double and led him to one side. Carl watched them in puzzlement, then turned to Terry as if asking for an explanation.

"It's a long story," Terry said. "One of Millard's experiments."

"Oh…I see." Carl pondered that for a moment. "I should have known. What do we do now?" He stood over Shara, his workpad in hand.

Why are you asking me? she wanted to answer, but there was such a lost look on the man's face that she knew it wouldn't do any good.

She had just inherited Spell Realm, or if not her, then Millard. Probably both of them. The park was privately owned. There was no board of trustees, no stockholders. Of course, this possibility had always been at the back of her mind, but her father had been so vibrant that it hadn't ever been something she seriously considered.

There was no one in charge. No one but her.

Terry was saying something to her. The storm blew his words away. "What?" she asked.

"We need to get everyone inside!" he repeated.

With that, all her uncertainty dropped away. The plan that had been forming in her mind became clear.

Chapter 29

I budgeted for the Windford Shield when I made the plans for Spell Realm. Of course I did. The memory of what happened to Placers Planet was still fresh in everyone's mind.

But Halor objected. "It's fake science," he said.

"It doesn't work?"

"Nothing would survive a direct hit," Halor said. "But that's beside the point. It's a bad risk assessment. The chance of such a thing happening again in our lifetime is almost nil."

So I pulled the expense from the budget. It give us enough margin to create the dragon that even then I was convinced would make or break Spell Realm.

Of course, when Charles Windford himself showed up and offered his top-of-the-line shield in exchange for a lifetime membership in Spell Realm, I jumped on it. I didn't expect the old man to take up permanent residence in the park, but when I realized his intention, I wasn't above using it in our advertising.

After all, if Charles Windford thought we were safe, then how dangerous could we be? All of this was before the Windford Shield fell into disrepute as planet after planet finally figured the risk correctly and had buyer's remorse. By then, Charles Windford was the richest man alive—at least, until my husband surpassed him.

— Martinique Mansing

The Windford Shield had always been invisible, but now its borders were being buffeted by sprays of radiation, swirling, swarming as if trying to get inside. Beyond the shield, the large oaks, once thick with greenery, were now bare. The once lush lawn was yellow, the flowerbeds stripped of life, the skies dark red, illuminated by bolts of lightning.

Millard's invention, the Entangler, sat alone at the base of the steps, abandoned. He and his twin had joined Shara and Terry at the top of the steps, standing close together, heads bent toward each other, whispering. People gave them startled glances, but no one approached them.

Shara knew that it was up to her to get the people moving. "Get inside, everyone!" she shouted.

No one heard her above the noise outside. Terry joined her in shouting, to no avail. Finally, Carl Lundy took notice. He adjusted something under his chin, and when he said "Get inside, everyone!," his voice boomed out much like Halor's had earlier. Apparently, some Personages had loudspeaker apps that Shara hadn't known about.

"Get inside, everyone," he repeated. "We are going to be here for a while!"

They didn't need much coaxing. Soon, only Carl remained on the steps with Shara and Terry. He was shaking his workpad, frustrated. "Damn radiation is messing with everything!"

Carl's muttered voice was still amplified, so several of the last guests entering the castle looked over their shoulders.

"Let's get out of the storm, Carl," Shara shouted.

With one last look at the baleful weather, Carl reluctantly turned to go inside.

As they came through the doors, a man emerged from the crowd. At first, Shara didn't recognize him. He was tall, with white hair and sharp blue eyes.

Then she realized it was Charles Windford, not the vague, ancient codger whom she'd known from the time she was a little child, but rejuvenated. This was the man who had earned the billions that would have allowed him to live full time in Spell Realm even if it hadn't been free. It suddenly came home to Shara that the name of the device was the Windford Shield.

"How is the shield holding up?" the old man asked, his voice strong, not quavering in the slightest.

Carl hunched over his workpad and swiped the screen

several times. "I'm not sure," he said, his voice booming over the loudspeaker. He frowned, then reached up and turned the microphone off. When he continued, his voice was soft and uncertain. "We calculated we had twenty days before the shield broke down."

Charles gave him a keen look. "But this is happening faster than you predicted?"

"How did you know that?"

"It's what I do," Charles said. "Or…it's what I used to do. I think you may be underestimating the strength of the shield. I know people think I scammed them, but I always felt the danger was real. And of course, whatever planet I planned to live on would have the strongest shield of all. If you don't mind, I'll go below and check. After all, I installed the damn thing."

Carl looked up, his mouth open. "*You* installed it? That was fifty years ago!"

Charles simply raised his eyebrows as if to say, *So?*

A lightning bolt struck one of the tall oaks just outside. The quaking from its impact rippled through the force field as if looking for a way in.

Immediately inside the doors, in the front alcove, was the check-in desk, and to one side of it was the room where guests chose their Personages. Shara and Terry ducked into it, followed by Charles Windford and Carl. Millard and Mill trailed along, still whispering to each other. Shara overheard a few sentences, but they didn't make any sense to her. It was as if they were speaking in code.

Millard—at least, she thought it was Millard—spoke up. "We'll go with you, Mr. Windford, if you don't mind."

He glanced over at them. "I don't know what's going on here, but would one of you two young men turn off your mirror Personage? You're confusing me."

"Yes, sir," Millard—or Mill—said, not bothering to correct him.

Charles nodded and turned away.

Shara saw one of the twins go to the wall, pick out a Personage, and put it on. When he switched it to activation mode, he turned into a handsome knight, tall and broad-shouldered.

Meanwhile, Carl was examining the old inventor doubtfully. "Maybe I should go with you too."

"I'll take care of it, my dear fellow, with the help of young Millard," Windford said. "Nothing you can do."

Shara glanced at Carl. Windford seemed to be implying that only geniuses need apply.

Carl glanced down at his workpad, frowning.

"Let Mr. Windford and…Millard go on ahead," Shara said. "I need you here, Carl. I've got an idea."

"Very well," Charles said. He looked as if he found the end of world invigorating. "Come along, Millard. Even geniuses can learn something new."

The elevator took them only part of the way. A series of Flexstone steps continued to lead downward. Mill followed his doppelgänger and the old man down the narrow stairs. It was clear from the undisturbed layer of dust that no one had been down this way in a long time. The Flexstone in the walls glowed softly, enough for them to see their way.

"Shouldn't we be working on the Entangler?" Mill whispered to his Other.

Millard was ahead of him, facing downstairs. The Flexstone must have been muffling noise somehow, because when he muttered something, Mill couldn't hear him. "What did you say?"

Millard turned and shouted, "It won't do us much good if the shield isn't working! Besides, I've never seen the inside of a Windford device. I'm curious."

Mill shook his head. The end of the world was happening outside, and his doppelgänger was…curious. *If I am anything like this, no wonder Master Lumbli loses patience with me!*

Then again, Charles Windford had a familiar look. Dress him in robes and he could be wizard of Munsury. All at once, Mill was as curious as his Other.

The steps became narrower and then began to spiral. The walls turned from smooth Flexstone to raw stone. Now the light came from bare lightbulbs strung from stapled wires. It grew hotter, and the steps started to get slippery as moisture dripped off the walls. The old man began to flag. Once, Millard had to reach out and steady him to keep him from toppling over the side of the stairs.

"We should rest," Mill said, but neither of his companions responded. "Stop!" he shouted.

Millard turned curiously, and it was only then that the old man slowed down, looking over his shoulder.

"I'm fine," Windford said. "We have no time to rest."

They started off again. But when Millard put a steadying hand on Windford's shoulder, the old man didn't object.

The steps widened and became straight. Mill sensed they were reaching the bottom. There was one last turn, onto a straight and level corridor.

Windford finally stopped to rest, breathing deeply and looking pale. "This is the bottom of the deepest crevasse I could find. The shield uses the raw material around it to amplify its effect."

He started shambling uncertainly forward, almost as if he couldn't see. Millard moved beside him and took his arm.

The corridor ended at a huge door, made of old-fashioned iron. It was the first man-made structure that Mill had seen that was Flexstone.

Windford pulled a chain from around his neck. A skeleton key hung from the silver links. "I chose not to use Flexstone for my device," he said as he inserted the key. There was a loud click, and the door swung open an inch. With some difficulty, the old man got his fingers around the edge and pulled the heavy door outward.

"Why?" Millard asked.

"Flexstone was new, and I didn't trust it. Besides, I wanted every world to have the shield, even those that couldn't afford Flexstone. Contrary to rumor, I charged each world only what it could afford."

The room was wide but shallow. The opposite wall consisted of dials and screens. Only the large dial in the middle was lit. There was a low hum, and the floor vibrated slightly. Windford strode across the room, and then reached out as if to steady himself. His palm landed on the center dial, and the vibration under their feet increased and the hum became louder until there was a grinding screech.

Windford slapped the dial again, and the grinding stopped. The walls lit up, each of the screens turning bright, the dials quivering.

"I told them to do this every few years," he muttered. "It never occurred to me that they wouldn't. But no harm done, apparently. I built this thing solid."

He moved to the side of the room where there was a narrow steel door. "Now…let's see what we see." He turned the latch and opened the door. Inside was a labyrinth of ceramic boxes, each marked with an infinity symbol, a sideways number 8.

Windford stepped back with a satisfied smile. "Good. No one has touched them. I told them it would ruin the warranty, but what I didn't say was that unless you open them just right, they'll stop working. I made half my money from worlds that didn't obey my instructions and had to be rebooted."

"What are they?" Millard asked.

"Quantum computers, each and every one. They have to be connected in precisely the right way. Get one out of order, and they all stop working. Shall we get started?"

"What are you going to do?" Mill asked.

The word "quantum" was the only one he understood completely. Only wizards endeavored to use Quantum Spells, the most dangerous and complex of all enchantments. Lumbli had only begun to train him on their uses, but Mill had already shown a natural aptitude that had impressed his master.

"This device has a little bit extra," Windford said, bending down and opening the largest of the ceramic boxes at the bottom. The other infinity signs were a dark blue, but this box had a bright red symbol. Inside were tiny coils and colored wires as thin as human hair. The terms "coils" and "wires" were new to Mill—he had read about and seen diagrams of them in the library that very morning.

"We use that sign in our magic," Mill said. "We call it the Infinity Spell."

"Magic?" Windford laughed. "Fair enough. I never quite understood it myself. I stumbled across the solution, but damned if I could explain it. It has to do with spooky action at a distance is all I know. I was working on quantum entanglement at the time."

Millard exchanged a sharp look with Mill. His invention uses much the same idea, Mill remembered, which is why the machine was called the Entangler.

Windford leaned forward and pressed the tip of the skeleton key against a small tab at the base of the large box.

The device's lights flickered; the hum intensified yet again. Windford straightened with a satisfied smile. "This is the strongest shield I ever built—twice as strong as any other." His voice quavered from the steady vibrations. "I considered it a challenge to build something that would withstand even a superluminous supernova."

Millard was staring at the device as if trying to memorize the impossible maze inside. "Is it supposed to be doing that?" he asked.

Windford bent down and grunted. A blue light was curling in and out of the wires. The room shook, and there was a loud clank.

All the lights went out.

Chapter 30

Spell Realm has felt real to me from the moment I first conceived it. Every detail has made it only more real. It is almost as if this world exists in a time and place just beyond my grasp. It has always felt more like the fulfillment of a dream than a creative act. Perhaps all creation is just that, borrowing from another dimension, seeing things that exist outside our view.

And if that is so, somewhere there is someone dreaming of this reality, thinking it a fantasy. If there are infinite possibilities, there are infinite worlds. I have chosen one that is comfortable for me, and I must hope that others will find it as endearing. It has all the virtues of real life without any of the drawbacks. In the real world, we age, we have limits, we suffer and get sick and die.

Here, there are no limits, no one need age, and no one should suffer.
That is what we offer in Spell Realm.

— Martinique Mansing

Shara watched Millard and his twin enter the elevator behind Mr. Windford. She shook her head. They were up to something. It wasn't like Millard—or Mill, probably—to volunteer to help with anything. Then again, they were going to die if something didn't change. It wasn't as if they could make things worse.

Right?

She turned to find Terry and Carl waiting. She took a deep breath, certain the two of them would shoot down her plan. "We've been going about the evacuation all wrong."

Terry nodded. Carl put aside his workpad and waited for

her to continue.

"We've been stupid, trying to take people to the spaceships. Instead, we should be bringing the spaceships to us."

"It's against the rules," Carl said automatically, then shook his head as he realized how silly that sounded.

"We have to get to the ships," she said. "All we need is one pilot to succeed. Once there, we can shuttle the rest of the ships back here one by one."

"It's a smart plan," Carl said. "But how do you get the first pilot over?"

Shara hadn't figured that part out yet. She just knew there had to be a way. "Do we have anything that can make it over the gorge?"

Carl stared at her helplessly.

"What about Humbert?" Terry said.

"Humbert?" Carl answered. "He isn't designed to carry people. In fact, Martinique Mansing insisted that not happen."

"But you can override his programming, can't you?" Shara asked.

"I suppose," Carl said, looking down at his workpad. "That is, if Humbert responds at all. He's affected by the Fanchon Particles like the rest of the Flexstone. Maybe more so."

"We have to try," Shara said. "Humbert may be our only hope."

Shaking his head, Carl turned back to his workpad.

"Humbert isn't answering," Carl said. "The walls of Castle La Magie may be interfering." He slapped the workpad in frustration, then looked closely to see if he'd done any damage.

Part of Terry was amazed that his boss was calling the dragon by his nickname, and part of him was trying desperately to think of where Humbert might be hiding. The Darke Dragon was usually either flying high above Spell Realm, an ever-present advertisement by the most popular creature in the park, or, more often than not, ensconced in his hangar, being repaired.

"Maybe the signals aren't reaching him," Shara said.

Terry was glad that she was finally taking charge. After

watching Mill and Millard disappear into the bowels of the castle, she'd been distracted, hardly aware of the ever-growing storm that buffeted the shield's force field.

"Give me one of the radiation suits," Carl said. "I'll go outside the shield and see if I can get through."

Shara looked down doubtfully at the suit she was wearing. "I don't think it will fit you," she said. The other functional radiation suit lay crumpled on the floor near the front desk. If anything, that suit was even smaller—far too tight a fit for a man of Carl Lundy's bulk.

Shara said, "Since I'm already wearing a radiation suit, why don't you give me the workpad and show me how to signal Humbert?"

"That's a terrible idea," Terry blurted. Just then, the entire castle shook; pictures fell off the walls, and chairs stuttered across the floor. It should have been impossible. Terry had once seen the schematics of Spell Realm in his boss's office; the entire edifice was built solidly on bedrock.

Carl shook his head. "Wearing a radiation suit or not, it's not safe. I'm not letting Halor Mansing's daughter kill herself on my watch."

"You have no choice, Mr. Lundy," Shara said. "I'm your boss now. If you don't tell me how, Terry will."

Terry went over and stood next to Carl. "I don't think so, Shara. I'm with Carl on this one."

She glared at them, and Terry almost gave in. But then the castle shook again, the ground shifting under their feet. He looked up to see the towers above them swaying. That gave him an idea.

"We could try signaling from the top of Founders Tower," he said. The tallest tower of Castle La Magie was at the exact geographical center of Spell Realm. If they couldn't reach Humbert from there, the dragon was probably lying broken amid some wreckage somewhere.

"How do we do that?" Carl asked. "It's locked tight." Halor Mansing's quarters in the Founders Tower were off limits even to employees as important as the chief engineer.

"I can get us in," Shara said.

Carl stared at her for a moment, and then said, "Of course you can."

Shara's expression softened. She leaned forward and put her hand on Carl's arm. "I appreciate that you pretended not to know me all this time, Carl." She managed to give him a slight smile, even in the midst of the disaster. "But we don't have time for that anymore. Someone has to take charge, and I guess that's me."

"Lead the way, boss," Carl said.

People stood aside as they went through the hallways. On the second floor, they met Granger Hovey. He looked even more cadaverous than usual, with sweat on his forehead as if he was melting from inside. Kirrie, next to him, was practically holding him up.

Shara motioned them over. Granger came over reluctantly, with Kirrie pulling on his hand.

"Yes, Ms. Mansing?" Granger said.

Terry winced. If more proof was needed that things had changed, it was this. Granger had always been a little too openly contemptuous of everyone, as if knowing who Shara really was had shielded him from retribution. Now he was deferential.

"I need you to lead our guests to the lower levels—as far down as you can take them," Shara said. "It may be safer down there."

Granger gulped and nodded.

"We'll see that it's done," Kirrie said, bowing slightly.

Shara continued down the hall, her eyes straight ahead, but Terry could see she was affected by the kowtowing. No matter what else happened, she'd never be able to pretend to be a mere servant again.

She led them to the third floor, and there she turned aside into an alcove that Terry had never paid much attention to. He'd always assumed the door there was a linen closet for the house-keeping staff.

They entered a small elevator, which shot upward so fast that Terry's knees bent. Shara had her eyes closed, and she looked pale. Terry took her hand. She looked up at him with a tentative smile.

"I'm sorry about your father," Terry said.

Meanwhile, Carl stared resolutely at the elevator door, but he appeared to be near tears.

The door opened on Halor Mansing's private office, something no one except Shara ever saw. The lights went on. The office was messy, with papers strewn across the desk as if its master had only just left but would return at any moment. Books lined most of the walls, with knickknacks filling the open spaces on their shelves. It was the same kitsch that Spell Realm sold to tourists, only these were the original prototypes: knights on stallions, wizards, unicorns, dragons.

Shara walked into the room and past the desk without looking around. There were curtains on the wall to the right of the desk, and she drew them aside to reveal an opening to a set of spiral stairs, which she marched up. At the top, a door opened onto a balcony that ringed the top of the tower. Instead of being greeted by sunshine, it was nearly dark outside, except for the streaks of red that swirled around them on all sides. In the distance, the Mossy Forest appeared to be on fire. The pavilions of the tournament grounds had blown away, leaving shattered beams and kindling. Toward the spaceport, the gleam of the ships couldn't be seen. Terry wondered if they were already submerged in the rising waters.

The shield's border appeared to be only inches above them, the narrow needle that topped the tower extending beyond it.

Lightning struck the needle, and Terry closed his eyes against the blinding flash of light.

"Everyone all right?" Carl said.

"We're safe here," Shara said. "As safe as anywhere in Castle La Magie. Mother made sure of that. The whole castle is on bedrock."

And sure enough, the tower hadn't shaken with the lighting strike, nor did it feel as if it was unsteady. The swaying Terry had noticed while below appeared to have been an illusion.

"This is as close to the shield as we can get," Shara said. "See if you can summon Humbert."

Carl brought out his workpad, gave a single swipe of the hand, and lowered it.

"I could've done that," Shara said, sounding aggrieved.

"If you only knew," Carl said, not the least bit apologetic.

"Let me have a look?" Terry asked.

Carl handed over the workpad, ostentatiously keeping it out of Shara's reach. She snorted in response.

"The signal is reaching *something*," Terry said. There was no real way of telling, but he'd called Humbert so many times that he recognized the wavelengths. He was pretty sure that the dragon was still receiving—but whether Humbert could respond was a different question.

"What if we don't get to the spaceport?" Shara asked. "Can we survive?"

Carl shook his head. "Mr. Windford may be a genius, and he may have built the strongest shield ever, but nothing can withstand the direct flare of a Fanchon burst. There are many who believe that's why we haven't run into alien races—that before a civilization has gotten as far as space flight, they've been wiped out."

"But the rest of humanity will be OK?" Shara asked.

"As long as they aren't in the path of the flare."

"Then humanity will go on without us," she whispered.

The signal on the workpad bleeped. Carl reached out for it, and Terry handed it back to him.

"Humbert's coming," Carl said.

As the words came out of his mouth, a shadow passed overhead. For the first time, the tower trembled. Humbert swooped past them, circling, then landed with a whoosh, his claws clutching the thin spire that rose overhead. He was outside the shield—which should have been impossible. The Fanchon Particles should have fried his circuits long ago, Terry thought.

Humbert flapped his wings, stabilizing himself, and his long neck twisted around and he stared at them. The dragon's scales were bright red, reflecting the skies. His claws and teeth were jet black.

One look into those eyes and Terry was certain that this wasn't the Humbert he knew. There was curiosity in them, and a hint of danger. This was the Darke Dragon—or what the Darke Dragon was meant to be.

"Can you hold him there?" Terry shouted. He looked for a way to climb the ramparts and onto the dragon's back. He'd done it before, once, when the Flexstone dragon was down for repairs, certain he would be fired if Carl happened to catch him.

There was a space just behind the dragon's head where a human could sit. That couldn't be an accident. Martinique Mansing may have forbidden riding Humbert, but she had nevertheless allowed for the possibility.

Carl looked over at Terry, panic in his eyes. He held his workpad out at arm's length as if it was foreign object. "I don't know. I don't recognize any of these readings."

"What do you think you're doing, Terry?" Shara said.

He turned toward her. This was going to be the most important argument of his life. "Humbert knows me best."

"That's not Humbert, and you know it. Besides, unless you know how to fly one of the ships, it's pointless."

"There might be something of old Humbert in there," Terry argued. "It's our best chance. I'll figure out the flying part."

"This is my responsibility," Shara said, shaking her head. "These people are here because of this world my parents created. I'll do it. It has to be me."

"Well, one of you better get to it," Carl said, motioning toward the dragon. Humbert was looking toward the ground as if something had caught his eye.

"Humbert!" Terry shouted. The great beast turned his head toward him. Terry put his hands on the bannister and started to climb, trying not to look down. The chill of vertigo went through his chest.

"You'd best listen to your boss."

Terry almost slipped at the voice, for it was one he didn't recognize. He lowered himself back to the balcony and turned.

Three young women had come through the door behind them. Despite their different-colored hair and clothing, they were identical.

"Who the hell are you?" Carl said.

"Honored guests of Spell Realm, aren't we, sisters?" the darkest of the women said. "You weren't planning on leaving us behind, were you? We'll have to lodge a complaint."

"You should go below," Shara said, sounding surprisingly calm. "It is safer there."

"Safer?" the blonde one said. "And yet, here you are."

Terry turned and started climbing again. He instinctively understood that these women weren't simply lost guests. Someone grabbed him from behind, and he found himself falling. He cried out, unsure which side of the rampart he was falling on. He slammed onto the balcony.

The blonde woman leaned over him and patted him on his cheek. "Not so fast, buster."

Chapter 31

Spell Realm only needs to provide half the illusion necessary for the fantasy to work. We humans appear to have a bottomless capacity for anthropomorphizing anything that looks even the slightest bit alive. Of course, we try to bridge the gap with as believable creatures as we can create.

If robots ever do gain sentience, it won't take long for us to adopt them as part of our family, the same way we do cats or dogs.

Or perhaps the robots will adopt us…

— Martinique Mansing

Terry struggled for breath. Shara knelt down next to him. To her relief, he managed to get to his knees, then to his feet.

Shara closed her eyes, going through the mental list of guests who'd arrived that week. She had an almost photographic memory for this; she could remember every guest's name, at least for a few days. The intruders had to be the three sisters from Morgana—the same planet that Caleb Chance had come from.

I knew there was something wrong with that man! Somehow, this is connected.

These had to be the Mayerlings, Trina, Marie, and… Shara struggled for third name, and then she had it: Selene.

"Go ahead, get on the dragon's back, Shara," one of the sisters said. She wasn't wearing make-up, and her hair was a mousy brown that was likely the triplets' natural color. "We're coming with you."

"That's crazy!" Terry objected.

"This isn't necessary, Miss Mayerling," Shara said. From

the woman's surprised reaction, she'd correctly guessed their identity.

"That's very good, Shara. I'm impressed. I'm Selene. The blonde bimbo there is my sister Marie. The overly dramatic goth is Trina. At your service."

"If you've studied me, then you must know I'm coming back…for everyone," Shara said.

"Oh, I don't doubt it. But even if you do, it doesn't matter. Our mission was about you, and we're leaving with you alone."

"Whatever your mission was, it can't be that important now," Carl Lundy objected. He reached out with a beefy hand to pull Selene away from Shara.

She whirled, drawing a knife from beneath her ranger's jerkin. "Back off."

Carl retreated, hands in the air. "What do you want?"

"As we said, to get the hell out of here," said Marie.

"And to take Miss Mansing with us," Trina said.

"Might as well get paid for our trouble," said Selene.

"Why?" Shara asked.

The three sisters exchanged quick glances. "Frankly, we are never told the *why* of our missions," Trina answered. "But if I had to guess, I'd say that perhaps your parents shouldn't have been so secretive about Flexstone. Perhaps they should have shared it with the rest of the Thousand Planets. At least one of those planets has apparently decided it's time that everyone have the secret."

"But don't you see?" Shara said. "It doesn't matter now. Spell Realm isn't going to survive this."

Trina sneered at her. "Are you telling me that *you* don't have the formula? That Daddy's little girl wasn't given her inheritance?"

Shara didn't answer—which was answer enough.

"Get on up there, Shara," Trina said. "Or do we have to start hurting your friends?"

Terry looked as if he was ready to fight. Marie stood close to him. Meanwhile, Trina had moved behind Carl, knife in hand.

"Please, this isn't necessary," Shara protested. "I swear to you, I'm coming back."

"Maybe you are, maybe you aren't," Selene said. "And maybe it'll be too late. Besides, the secret is out; we've rather revealed ourselves here. I doubt you're just going to let this go, are you?"

Again, Shara didn't answer.

"Go on ahead, Shara," Terry said. He knew it would be impossible for her to tell a convincing lie. "We'll wait here."

Shara looked into Terry's eyes and nodded. "I'll be back for you, I promise."

The Darke Dragon had been watching from his perch, curious, as if he understood what was being said. When Shara climbed to the top of the parapet, the dragon dipped his head downward slightly, allowing her to scramble onto his back. Humbert's head was covered with lumpy growths, and she grabbed a couple of them. The scales beneath her legs were rough, helping hold her in place. Shara could feel the dragon's muscles moving under his skin—this was no machine, but a living, breathing creature. How was she supposed to control him? Or would Carl be able to direct Humbert with his workpad?

Selene climbed up behind her and put one arm around her waist. Shara felt something sharp against one side of her neck and heard a whisper in the opposite ear. "Don't try anything."

Trina climbed up next, sitting behind her sister. Humbert craned his neck at them, as if objecting to the weight.

Marie was last. She stood on the top of the parapet, seemingly unfazed by the long drop behind her, and looked down at Carl and Terry. "Behave yourselves, you two. If you're lucky, maybe we'll send your dragon back. After we've made our escape, of course."

Marie climbed up, the dragon watching her. She sat behind the other three women, barely fitting in the space between Humbert's head and the crest at the base of his neck.

Sensing that they were ready, Humbert lifted off, pushing away from the spire and dropping with gut-wrenching swiftness toward the ground. A downward stroke of his wings pushed his riders down against his neck. One of the sisters cried out, but whether from fear or exaltation, Shara couldn't tell. She was feeling both emotions in equal measure herself.

The dragon flew low over the roofs of Castle La Magie, then past the tournament grounds and toward the burning forest.

Wrong direction.

Shara pulled hard on the horny growth she clutched in her right hand, and in response, the dragon turned to the right. She tried the other hand, and Humbert turned to left. A thrill went through her. It was as if she'd done this before, as if riding a dragon was her birthright.

They flew over Castle La Magie again. Terry and Carl still stood on the balcony, watching. Shara dared to lift her right hand. *I'll be right back*, her wave promised. The dragon seemed to sense the shield's borders, flying just below its blurred outline. In minutes, they had flown over the same terrain Shara had traveled all that morning, struggling to move a few footsteps at a time.

They reached the chasm. Shara forced herself to look down, hoping that, by some miracle, there would be some sign of her father. All she could see were the raging torrents of whitewater and the crumbling cliffs. Half the spaceships were gone, swept away by the rising waters. The other half were on higher ground but awash and tilting, and it wouldn't be long before they too were gone.

Humbert instinctively flew toward the largest ship and landed awkwardly, his claws scrabbling for purchase against the wet rock.

Marie slid off the dragon's back and made her way to the spaceship. Trina slid down next, but Selene hesitated. The point of her knife dug into Shara's neck. Blood trickled down, mixing with the rain.

Selene said, "We go together."

"No," Shara said. "You can escape, but you're not taking me with you."

"My dear girl, you're the only reason we're here. We aren't leaving without you. If I have to cut you, I will. Those were our instructions: capture if possible, kill if not. We only get half as much for you dead, so I'd rather not kill you. But if you disobey, I won't hesitate."

"You'd let hundreds of people die? And you still would get the formula?"

"Of course," Selene said, her voice calm.

"I'll pay you twice whatever you were offered," Shara said. "Four times whatever my death is worth to you."

"You will, will you?" Selene laughed. "No! We have our reputations to consider. Now come along before we all get swept away."

Shara shook her head. She could barely form the words, but they came out. "I'd rather die."

"Have it your way," Selene said.

Shara closed her eyes, waiting for the cut, wondering how much it would hurt. She felt Humbert spreading his wings, the wind of their passage ruffling her hair. And then she was pushed down in her seat, her hands nearly coming off their holds. The knife slid down the side of her neck, scraping but not penetrating far.

Selene cried out, her one-armed grip around Shara's waist coming loose.

By the time Shara opened her eyes, there was emptiness behind her. Selene was falling, hitting the ground and sliding against the rock. She came to a stop and lay there, unmoving. Her sisters turned and ran toward her, then, looking up at the dragon in alarm, reversed course and sprinted toward the spaceship.

Humbert whirled and swooped down on them. Too late, Shara realized the dragon's intentions.

"No, Humbert!"

Her words were drowned out by the whoosh of flame. The two sisters were engulfed as fire flowed across the rock, catching them in midstep. The flames continued to flow, reaching one of the spaceships, which exploded.

Humbert turned so swiftly that Shara barely held on. She heard the whizzing of metal fragments flying over her head. As Humbert flew over the chasm, Shara looked back. Another spaceship exploded, and she closed her eyes against the shockwave. When she opened them again, the last of the ships had disappeared.

There was nothing but stone and water.
Their last chance at escape was gone.

Chapter 32

It may seem strange, but when Halor and I started Spell Realm, neither of us had any belief in magic or in the supernatural. We searched the legends and myths of Earth for our creatures and stories.

But as they came alive within Spell Realm, I started to see how there was truth to all these stories, and it made me wonder. Perhaps, once upon a time, magic really did exist. How else could everything we've created seem so real?

— Martinique Mansing

The lights flickered back on.

Mill turned toward Mr. Windford expectantly. "How do we activate your booster?"

Mr. Windford stared back at him, his eyes unfocused. He was hunched over, unsteady on his feet. His hand flexed as if he was reaching for a cane. "What's that, young man? Why are we down here? I'm retired. I don't do this anymore."

Mill exchanged an alarmed look with Millard, who went to the old man's side and took his arm. "We are in the middle of a Fanchon Particle burst, Mr. Windford. Remember? We need to strengthen your shield."

"Nonsense," Windford said. "There is no such thing. All my shields are the same."

"What's wrong with him?" Mill asked.

"He's very old. His longevity treatments are starting to fail."

"How old is he?" Mill tried to keep the amazement out of his voice. At first, he'd thought this world was backward. Imagine not having spells to magically do any of the work! But the longer he was here, the more he realized that this world's science had created a civilization that far exceeded any magic he'd ever heard of. At the same time, he recognized the class structure of this world: the wealthy benefited the most from science, just as on his world, the nobility benefited the most from magic.

"If I remember rightly, Windford was an old man when Placers Planet was destroyed," Millard said. "That was over fifty years ago. He invented his device soon after. He must be well over a hundred and thirty-five years old, at least."

"We don't have any magic that can do that," Mill said, shaking his head. He turned toward the panel, examining the maze of ceramic boxes. The biggest box at the bottom of the array stood out, its infinity sign colored a bright red. At the center of the sign was a button.

"He pushed that," Mill said, pointing.

"Yes, and the power went out shortly after. Do we dare try it again?"

"What choice do we have?" Mill said.

Millard gently took the key from Windford and handed it to Mill. He leaned down and pressed the key against the tab.

The lights flickered but didn't blink out again. The lights in the big box, however, blinked off. The other parts of the shield were still working—or at least, Mill assumed they were, otherwise they'd be dead by now.

They both turned to Windford, hoping the man with the sharp blue eyes who had led them down here had returned.

Windford swayed from side to side, and a moan escaped his lips.

"Do you have any idea how to fix this?" Mill asked.

"How could I?" Millard exclaimed. "It's a black box. It makes no sense to me."

Mill bent down again and examined the wires and coils. It was a machine made with technology completely foreign to him, and yet...

He straightened up. "We'll have to use the Entangler, try to shift this world even more toward mine. My world isn't threatened by these Fanchon Particles."

Millard closed his eyes, frowning. Then he nodded slightly. "We might be able to send a few of us to your world. We need to go find Shara and Terry…maybe Mr. Lundy."

"You go on ahead," Mill said. "Take the old man with you. I'll catch up."

"What are you going to do?" Millard asked.

"I'll tell you if it works," Mill said. "Get going."

Carl Lundy and Terry waited for Shara on the balcony. Carl's head was down, his fingers moving over his workpad, his shoulders hunched in frustration. Humbert landed on the spire, flapping his wings to stay steady while Shara climbed down onto the rampart. Then the dragon sprang into the air, the spire reverberating behind him. He flew into the storm and disappeared.

Terry took Shara's hand to help her down. "What happened?"

"They're gone," Shara said. Her voice sounded numb, lifeless. "Everything's gone, the whole spaceport."

Carl threw his pad onto the hard Flexstone, and it shattered. "The damn thing is useless. Nothing works!"

"What do we do now?" Terry asked.

Shara shook her head. "We have to hope that Millard can think of something. His invention changed this world. Humbert isn't a machine anymore, he's real."

"Real?" Carl repeated.

"I think the magic of Mill's world has entered ours," Shara said. "Perhaps our science has invaded his world too, I don't know. But it will take some kind of magic to save us now. Have Millard and Mill returned from the Windford Shield?"

"I don't know," Terry said. "The shield is still holding, so maybe they've strengthened it."

"Who's Mill?" Carl demanded. "Mill's world? What is going on?"

Terry turned to his boss. He had to shout to be heard; the storm had intensified, and the borders of the shield were bending alarmingly. "Millard invented a machine that crosses dimensions. His twin from that world crossed over, and it looks like the rules of our universe have changed. Mill, the doppelgänger, calls it magic."

"Magic? What are you two talking about?" Carl said. "There's no such thing as magic. It's all an illusion."

"Not anymore," Shara said. "We need to find Millard, and Mill, too." She headed toward the stairs, not waiting for a response.

The hallways of Castle La Magie were empty. Apparently, Granger and Kirrie had succeeded in getting everyone down below. When they reached the lobby, Shara headed for the elevators across from them.

The elevator doors opened. Millard, or Mill, stepped out, guiding Mr. Windford, who appeared dazed. Shara decided it was Millard, because his twin usually had an inquisitive look on his face.

"Mr. Windford is having one of his episodes," Millard said. "But before he went into his stupor, he showed us a booster he installed to the shield. It failed." He gave Shara a forlorn look. "From the look on your face, you didn't succeed either."

"The ships are gone," Shara said. She shook her head. No point in mentioning the Mayerling sisters.

"There is one more thing we can try," Millard said. "If it was possible for Mill to move into our universe, it should be possible for us to cross into his, at least, for a few of us."

Shara stared at him blankly. "I'm not leaving everyone else here, if that's what you're thinking."

Terry started to say something but thought the better of it, realizing from her determined expression that she wouldn't be dissuaded.

"We'll take as many people as we can," Millard said. "I have no idea what reach we will have. The only way to find out is to try."

Shara hesitated, as if suspecting a trick. "We'd best bring up as many people as we can, then."

Mill waited until his doppelgänger and the old man left the room before reaching down and taking hold of the ceramic box with the red infinity sign.

Either this works or we all die, he thought.

He pulled the box out of the array and held his breath.

Again, the lights flickered but stayed on. The other boxes
continued to hum. Mill didn't know what the Fanchon Particles
would do to him, but he suspected it would be quick but
unpleasant.

After a few moments, Mill allowed himself a deep breath.
He held the box gingerly. It was warm in his hands, and a tin-
gling sensation went through his body—the same kind of prick-
ling he got from weaving a powerful enchantment.

Mr. Windford calls this science, Mill thought. *But it looks like
magic to me.*

He left the room and started up the steps, holding the box
carefully in front of him. By the time he reached the elevator, he
had been joined by a crowd of people, the youngest of whom
brushed by him on their way upward. Several times, he was jos-
tled so hard that he almost dropped the infinity box. The crowd
in front of the elevators was too thick for Mill to get through.

A tall man near the edge of the crowd turned and saw Mill
coming. His eyes opened wide. Beside him stood a woman he
recognized. Even though it had only been a day since he'd left
her, it seemed like an eternity.

"I need to get through, Kirrie," Mill said through gritted
teeth.

"Gangway!" the tall man shouted. "Let Millard through.
Move aside!"

Mill kept walking, hoping they would let him by. Reluctantly,
one by one, people moved to either side. Mill reached the elevator doors just as they were opening.

No one else joined him. The doors closed. The elevator shot
upward so fast that Mill almost lost hold of the box, which was
beginning to feel heavy. Reluctantly, he pulled the box closer to
his body. It was a shock, and the tremor that had been running
through his fingers and hands now rumbled through the rest
of his body.

He clenched his chattering teeth. *Spellshine.* This is what the
deadly enchantments of his own world felt like.

At least it's powerful, Mill thought. *We'll need all the magic we
can get.*

Chapter 33

It came as a surprise to me that so many of our visitors believe that the creatures we have concocted are real. Well, perhaps not these very creatures, but many seem to believe that such mythological beings really exist.

Even more surprising, they expect me and Halor to be believers. Why else would we have created such a place?

Halor sees Spell Realm as an experiment, whereas for me, it has simply been an expansion of my childhood love for legends and myths.

More than one visitor to Spell Realm has reported seeing animals and beings that are not on our roster. We don't have elves or dwarves, for instance, but more than one guest has come back from the Mossy Forest to report having had interactions with such beings.

After some consideration, I decided not to disabuse them of their fanciful notions.

— Martinique Mansing

Mill finally worked his way through the crowded lobby and onto Castle La Magie's front steps. Millard stood, chin in hand, staring at the Entangler as if he'd never seen it before. Behind him, Carl was laying out his tools on the first stair, one by one, with Terry looking on. Charles Windford was sitting on the second stair, chatting conversationally about the weather. Judging by his smile and blank look, the old man was still not in full possession of his wits.

Shara was holding a flashlight on the machine.

Mill was relieved and somewhat surprised to see her. In Munsury, only master wizards rode dragons. But though she had survived the experience, she had obviously failed in her mission.

The Entangler sat just inside the borders of the shield, a few feet from the steps. Outside the shield was a swirl of red and black. The shield's surface was bulging alarmingly. The noise was muted, and yet the rising thrum made it clear that the storm was getting worse by the second.

As Mill came closer, he saw that the Entangler was lopsided, one of its legs broken, parts askew, with loose wires dangling from the contraption.

Millard stepped toward his device, lifted a loose wire, then let it go and stepped back, confused. "I can't remember," he muttered. "I thought I knew where everything went." Millard turned his head, saw Mill coming toward him, and said, "I think we may be missing a part."

"Do you have a diagram?" Shara said. "A blueprint of some kind?"

"I didn't need one. Everything just seemed to fit, but now…" Millard took a long wire with a frayed end and held it up, then lifted another wire the same color and started to splice them together.

"No," Mill said, "it doesn't go there."

It was strange, but the convoluted maze of wires made sense to him now. It wasn't because of his time in the library. No, the patterns looked like magic to him—magic made physical. Instead of holding a formula in his mind or trying to trace the magic paths with his hands, it was as if thoughts had been made real.

Millard turned to him, the wires still in hand. Mill took the longer one from him and lifted it toward the crown of the machine, knowing exactly where it was meant to go.

"Yes, that's it," Millard said. "How did you know that?"

"He's you, isn't he?" Shara said. "He thinks like you."

This first connection jogged Millard's memory, and he started quickly attaching the others loose wires, straightening things, screwing down parts, and putting the Entangler back into the shape Mill remembered first seeing.

And yet it was still not quite right.

"Wouldn't it be better to have this piece here?" Mill asked, taking a loose spring and moving it to the opposite side.

Millard took the part from Mill's hand impatiently. "I know what I'm doing."

Behind them, people were starting to spill out of the lobby and onto the stairs. Terry faced them with his hands out and said, "Let them work, people. Keep back."

"What is that thing?" someone shouted.

"If you let us do our job, it might be our salvation," Terry said.

"Mr. Windford!" someone else shouted. "Are we going to be OK?"

Charles Windford stood and faced the crowd. "We are quite safe, I assure you. The Windford Shield will save us."

Mill watched Millard finish attaching the last of the loose parts. He stepped back as if he expected the machine to do something.

"Doesn't it need to be powered?" Shara asked.

"The batteries should still be good," Millard muttered.

He turned to Carl, who nodded.

"I'll be right back," Carl said. He pushed his way through the throng and disappeared.

Millard fussed with the Entangler, but he seemed to be out of answers.

Mill could sense the machine's underlying power. It was the same magic that was within the box he held, and the two objects were calling to each other.

When Millard turned away from the Entangler to grab a tool, Mill took his opportunity. The infinity box fit snuggly in a shelf just below the crown of the machine. Mill grabbed two of the wires crossing over the front and pulled them apart. He entwined them at the two ends of the box.

Blue flame zapped upward out of the machine, a bolt that struck the edge of the shield. For an instant, the shield seemed to disappear, and Mill saw the flames and smoke of what was left of Spell Realm outside. Then the few feet of shield around where it had been struck grew dark, as if becoming solid.

"What are you doing?" Millard cried out.

But the Entangler was already transforming. The wires and cables, controllers and circuits, platters and magnets were whirling in place, shifting, moving around the machine as if alive.

A blue glow suffused the Entangler, spreading outward, moving up the steps and pushing the borders of the shield outward. It was the same blue light that had surrounded Mill before he was transported to this world.

It was, perhaps, enough to save those few people within the circle of light.

Realizing what was happening, Shara climbed the stairs backward until she was beyond the blue light.

"Hurry, Lady Sharina…Shara!" Mill cried. "Come with us."

"I'm not leaving without everyone else," she shouted above the whir of the Entangler. Terry hurried to her side, took her hand, and tried to pull her after him. She pushed him away. He stood there uncertainly, then dropped his hands to his sides and joined her.

Millard appeared to have been paralyzed by both his invention's unexpected response and by Shara's words. Then it looked as if he was going to step out of the light too.

Mill couldn't allow that. He grabbed his twin by the arm.

From the corner of his eye, he saw the surface of the shield becoming opaque and then completely clear, the blue light extending farther and farther into the darkness.

The Entangler shook, throwing off sparks, and the infinity box glowed a bright red. And yet, it wasn't enough. There was still something missing. Millard pulled his arm out of Mill's grasp, his face red with anger.

From beyond the blue light, Mill saw the unicorn approaching. It was untouched by the devastation around it, glowing with its own white light.

The Majestic Ultima is the missing part of the enchantment, Mill thought. It had been there, in both worlds, when he crossed over into this one. The magic didn't work without it.

The unicorn stepped into the circle of blue light. There was a blinding flash. Mill pushed his doppelgänger away and fell to his knees. He was completely blind, and for an instant, he felt the Fanchon Particles flowing through him, and then he pitched forward into darkness.

Chapter 34

I have tried my best to make Spell Realm self-sustaining. We have our own crops and livestock, our own workshops and tradesfolk. It is my goal to have paying visitors be our only import.

Of course, it is impossible to make our own complex AIs and heavy machinery, but I have hope that even these items will one day be home-produced. Halor's mastery of Flexstone is becoming more sophisticated with every year that goes by.

The Thousand Worlds have become so interconnected that I fear most of them would not survive if they became isolated, though what could cause such an event is beyond imagination.

— Martinique Mansing

Lady Sharina.

Shara was having a hard time adjusting to the new title. She stood on her father's balcony looking down upon Spell Realm. Though the land looked the same as before the Fanchon Particle burst, it wasn't. Everything was different.

A shadow flew overhead, and she looked up in time to see the Darke Dragon disappearing behind the clouds. No one called the dragon by the nickname Humbert anymore. There was nothing lighthearted about the creature.

No one called the unicorn Horny, either. Most used the name Mill had called it: Majestic Ultima. Shara had been trying to catch a glimpse of the creature ever since that fateful day when science had been replaced by magic.

She looked at the clock on the wall. It was a mechanical device, built by Terry. Electricity and everything that ran on electricity didn't work. Well, most of the time it didn't work.

She had a couple of hours before the Ruling Council met again. She had time for her daily walk in the Mossy Forest. She took the stairs down to the lobby—now called the grand ballroom—of Castle La Magie. People stepped aside for her. It was a bunch of nonsense, but she put up with it because someone had to be in charge.

The Ruling Council. She shook her head at the grandiose description.

It wasn't long after magic arrived that Shara was forced to become Lady Sharina of Castle La Magie. Ruling power had been invested in her by her new subjects as soon as they realized that they were no longer guests, but full-time citizens of Spell Realm.

In truth, no one else wanted the job. Besides, she was the only one who understood all the inner workings of the castle.

Never mind that most of her inside knowledge was now useless, seeing as it was based on science and technology, which sometimes worked, but most of the time didn't. Instead, people were finding that other methods worked better—wish fulfillment, made-up enchantments, willpower. Might as well call it what it was—magic.

Millard was busy writing down what spells worked and what spells didn't.

Flexstone no longer worked by the formulas that Shara had been taught, but it was more susceptible to the new magic than most things.

When they'd gone to check the Windford Shield, they'd found a hole in the wall where it had been. Meanwhile, the Entangler had become something much bigger and more elaborate, encased in stone, its moving parts frozen, but giving off a constant thrum of power.

Some of the pieces of this new device looked a lot like the parts of the missing shield.

"How is that possible?" Shara had asked.

"I don't know," Millard said. "You'd have to ask Mill."

When they'd recovered from the blinding light of the shift, Mill had vanished—gone back to where he'd come from, they hoped.

"If this isn't *his* world," Terry asked, "then where are we?"

"I don't know," Millard shrugged. "It's magic."

It was clear that they were on their own. Not only were the spaceships gone, but none of their communications devices worked. In fact, almost everything technological had failed or was unreliable.

Charles Windford was useless. He was more doddering than ever, having lost whatever sharpness he'd managed to regain during the crisis. Terry and Carl were also struggling. They had relied on their technological know-how, and none of that mattered anymore.

Shara asked them to be part of the Ruling Council nevertheless, because she trusted them. Besides, it was impossible to explain to most of the onetime guests what had happened. All anyone knew was that the rules of the universe had changed overnight, and no amount of complaining or wishing was going to change that. This was their new reality.

Shara reached the castle doors. Kirrie North and Granger Hovey were at the front desk. For some reason, the two had proven to have an instinctive understanding of magic, and Shara had asked them to join the Ruling Council as well.

Granger hurried over. "Would you like an escort, milady?"

"No, thank you, Granger. I'm just going for a short walk. I'll be back in time for the meeting."

Granger looked doubtful. Outside the castle was now a dangerous place. The Mossy Forest had recovered and was filled with creatures that no one had ever seen before. Millard had taught Shara a few rudimentary defensive spells, so she felt safe enough.

Millard sometimes came to the council meetings. When he did, he sat uncomfortably close to Shara. He and Terry were no longer friends. Something had changed. Millard was more serious than before, and he seemed newly interested in Shara—not as a stepsister, but something else.

Shara skipped down the steps and strolled through what had once been the tournament tent grounds and now was a thriving market of trade goods and produce. People nodded to her as she passed; she'd made it clear that bows and curtsies weren't welcome.

The path into the Mossy Forest was starting to become over-grown, since most people avoided the dark woods. Shara wandered down it until she reached the small pond with the oak tree.

She felt safe there, for some reason. She sat with her back to the tree and closed her eyes, breathing in the smell of the trees and flowers. There was a rustling from the thick undergrowth behind her.

Shara opened her eyes but stayed still.

The Majestic Ultima moved into her line of sight. He approached slowly and stood over her for a few moments. Then he got to his knees and lay down next to her, gently lowering his head onto her lap.

She reached out and combed her fingers through his black mane.

The Ruling Council was going to meet shortly, but Shara was in no hurry. Without machines, everything had slowed down. Life was different with magic...and Shara wasn't sure it wasn't an improvement.

Millard will figure out how to use the magic, she thought.

The Majestic Ultima stirred at that thought and lifted his head, looking into her eyes as if trying to tell her something.

Millard was different, as if...

She shook her head. The unicorn rose to his feet and, with a whisk of his long tail, disappeared back into the forest.

Shara sighed, got up, and walked back toward Castle La Magie.

Epilogue

Millard woke in the middle of a grassy meadow. There was a small pond at its center, with a large oak tree hanging over the water.

He rose to his knees with a groan.

The last thing he remembered was Mill pushing him in the back. There'd been a blinding light, and then…nothing.

He heard someone humming and turned to see a man enter the clearing. He was wearing what appeared to be a wizard's costume, a blue gown covered by magical symbols and a conical hat. At first, Millard thought it was Carl Lundy, but as he drew closer, Millard could see he was thinner and older. Not a twin, but someone who'd served the same role in this world.

"There you are, Mill!" the man said. "I've been looking everywhere for you!"

Millard opened his mouth to object, but something made him keep quiet.

"Lady Sharina wants to see you," the man said.

"Lady Sharina?"

"Yes, yes, I know you've never met her, but for some reason she's taken a sudden interest in you. Come along, we're late." The man turned back down the path. For the first time, Millard looked up over the trees. In the distance, the towers of Castle La Magie rose into the sky, impossibly tall.

Mill had made it clear that his world was a dangerous place. No doubt he thought Millard wouldn't survive. He probably thought he'd won.

I'm in a world where magic is how things are done, not science. The quicker I learn, the better I'll survive. And when I've learned enough, I'll return to my world and show my doppelgänger who the real Millard is.

There's only room for one of us.

Millard followed the wizard.

About the Author

Duncan grew up and spent most of his life in Central Oregon, the dry side of the Cascades, and whose terrain is featured in many of his books. He wrote several books out of college, including the heroic fantasy novels Star Axe, Snowcastles, and Icetowers. In 1984, he and his wife Linda bought Pegasus Books in downtown Bend, Oregon, which they still own and operate. They also ran a used bookstore, the Bookmark, for 15 years.

In the last five years, he's been able to get back to writing again, and found that he has a lot of pent-up creative energy. He's written numerous books for several different publishers, mostly in the horror or dark fantasy genres, though recently has been branching out into fantasy again, as well as thrillers.

Curious about other Crossroad Press books?
Stop by our site:
http://store.crossroadpress.com
We offer quality writing
in digital, audio, and print formats.